DEAD DRIFT

Three Short Mystery Stories

S.W. Hubbard

Contents

Welcome to Trout Run....

Trout Run, NY is an idyllic and wholly fictional little town nestled in the High Peaks region of the Adirondack Mountains, somewhere between the real towns of Lake Placid and Keene Valley. Police Chief Frank Bennett is an outsider there--recently widowed and forced out of his detective position in the Kansas City police force. For fans who have already read the three Frank Bennett mystery novels, *The Lure*, *Blood Knot*, and *False Cast*, these short stories provide some new adventures with old friends. For those who are just getting acquainted with Frank in these stories, I hope you will continue on to read the three novels.

Chainsaw Nativity

The Thanksgiving turkey had not yet been served, but as soon as the first snow fell, signs of Christmas began popping up around Trout Run, New York. The ladies crafts circle hung an elaborate wreath on the door of the Presbyterian Church, while the bartender at the Mountainside strung tinsel over the beer kegs and mounted an erratically lighted sign that proclaimed MERR CH ISTMAS, a slurred Teleprompter for the patrons perched on his wobbly barstools. North Country Country 93.3 played Dwight Yoakum's "Here Comes Santa Claus" at least once an hour; every night a few more houses glowed with fairy lights. And, on the town green, Bucky Rheinholz's chainsaw Nativity was unveiled.

Frank Bennett dodged through the Nativity-viewing crowd, already dense at ten in the morning. He would have liked to pause and look at the statues again himself, but was already late for his meeting with Pastor Bob Rush. Charging into the church office out of breath, Frank saw he needn't have hurried. No Myrna at the front desk, no Bob in the pastor's study. Then, from the kitchen he heard voices.

"Yesterday the milk disappeared, today it's the sugar. I tell you, I can't put anything in this kitchen without it being carried off."

"You know they need it, Myrna. Just go buy some more." Frank came around the corner in time to see Bob pull ten bucks from his pocket.

"If they need help, all they have to do is ask. This is stealing, plain and simple."

"Problem?" Frank asked.

Myrna and Bob froze. "Nothing we need police help with, thank you anyway, Frank. Myrna's being called to do God's work."

Myrna took the cash and stalked out the door.

"Seems to be a little static interfering with His signal."

Bob smiled. "If everyone could hear the message loud and clear, I'd be out of a job. Now, tell me what you want to do about this traffic problem I've created."

They walked to the front door of the church as a tour bus from Albany pulled up to the green, disgorging fifty camera-toting senior citizens.

Frank had watched in amazement the week before as Bucky Reinholz and three burly men wrangled the well-wrapped pieces of the Nativity off a flat-bed truck borrowed from the lumberyard. Each statue was as big as the men who carried it, and by the time they had them all unloaded the crew was red-faced and sweating even in the brisk November air.

Frank had helped cut away the paper and padding protecting the figures and as each cover fell away, he grew more amazed. Chainsaw art cropped up all over the Adirondacks, in little souvenir shops, craft fairs, or set up on front lawns with hand-painted "for sale" signs. Mostly totem poles or bears sitting on their haunches--if you'd seen one, you'd seen them all.

Frank fell squarely into the "I don't know much, but I know what I like" school of art criticism, but even to his unschooled eye, Bucky Reinholz's chainsaw Nativity qualified as a masterpiece. The kneeling Mary radiated a tender joy; the shepherd looked curious and a little fearful; one of the three kings glanced skyward as if he wasn't sure that star could be trusted. The infant Jesus in his manger had been carved from an enormous stump, the baby emerging as if the tree itself had given birth.

Frank had wandered from statue to statue, entranced. Up close, the rough cuts of the chainsaw seemed to obliterate the figures' features, but when you took a few steps back you saw that the grooves themselves were what created their astonishingly lifelike expressions. The effect was magical, and Frank couldn't stop examining them.

"You did all this with a *chainsaw?*"

"A five horsepower Husqvarna, mostly," Bucky said.

"How long did it take?"

"Umm, close on to three years, I guess. Had a little trouble with the first baby Jesus. Wood wasn't fully dried, and after I had it all carved, I came out to the shop one morning and found it cracked right down the middle." Bucky grinned, revealing the large strong incisors that had given him his nickname.

Frank thought he seemed awfully good-natured about his setback. "Didn't it bother you to lose something you'd worked so hard on?" He'd built a pretty mahogany end table once, and a wild little friend of his daughter's had knocked it over and taken a big chunk out of it. He still bore that kid a grudge, twenty years later.

"Oh, no use to complain. Besides, the second one turned out even better."

"Are you going to move all this back to your shop after Christmas?"

Bucky slapped his thigh. "Hell, no. This is my gift to Trout Run. Pastor Bob and Ardyth Munger have some crazy notion it'll be a tourist attraction to raise money for the church."

And the crazy notion had proved true. Which brought them to today's problem. The chainsaw Nativity was attracting so many sightseers that traffic in the one-stoplight town was totally balled up. "Earl spends his whole day out here directing traffic," Frank complained to Pastor Bob. "The kid hasn't had a day off since the Nativity went on display."

8

"You're not suggesting we take it down, I hope?" Bob asked. "All the businesses in town are benefiting."

"No, no—I really like it, too. But could you organize some guys from the church to help with traffic control?"

"No problem. I'll pitch in myself if you think Earl will let me wear that orange reflective vest."

They strolled onto the green, wandering among the statues. This time, Frank took particular notice of the Joseph. Bucky had carved him sitting, gazing at his wife and the child. He looked stunned, as if he couldn't absorb what had happened to him. Frank remembered feeling that way himself in the delivery room, staring at Estelle and the wrinkled little bundle that was their daughter, Caroline.

"I think of all the statues, Joseph is my favorite."

"Yes, I like him too," Bob agreed. "Joseph is so underrated. Just think—his fiancée comes to him with this extraordinary story that she's pregnant, but still a virgin, and the child she's carrying is the son of God. And instead of casting her out to be stoned to death for adultery, he agrees to protect her and marry her and raise the child as his own." Bob touched the puzzled but trusting wooden brow of Joseph. "He believes Mary."

Frank continued to stare at the statue. Trust. Maybe that was what made the Joseph so unusual. Trust wasn't an expression you saw much on the face of a grown man. And Bucky had somehow captured that with his chainsaw. Go figure.

Crime in Trout Run peaked each week between 4PM on Friday afternoon when the men at Stevenson's Lumberyard received their paychecks, and 2AM on Saturday when they had drunk them half away at the Mountainside Tavern. Frank made a point of stopping by the Mountainside late every Friday night.

Tonight's crowd wasn't rowdy, but a certain edginess hung in the air. A group of men in hunters' camo sat at the bar complaining.

"Greg Haney's had my rifle for close on two weeks and he still don't have it fixed. What am I supposed to do, with buck season starting in three more days?"

"I don't care if he is a cripple—that just ain't right."

"I heard he kept Herb's shotgun for nearly a month."

"And what's more, when you call up to ask about it, he won't talk to you. Make's his girl say he can't come to the phone. Hides out behind his kids 'cause he knows I won't swear at them."

"I have half a mind to go out there and collect my gun. I don't care if it's in a million little pieces."

"Greg's a helluva gunsmith, but it seems like he can't keep up with the work since the accident."

The grousing continued, but since everyone agreed about Greg Haney's poor service, and the object of their complaint wasn't present, Frank left them to it. He checked out the action in the game room, where Ray Stulke was trying to hustle a pool game from two young men clearly marked as tourists by the lift tickets stuck to the zippers of their expensive ski jackets. They might as well have worn signs reading FLEECE ME. Frank sat down, estimating ten minutes for Ray to lure them into a double-or-nothing bet, three for him to sink every ball on the table, and thirty seconds for the fight to break out.

But the tourists were both better gamblers and better pool players than Frank gave them credit for, and Ray had to work hard to win. The game ended in laughter and back-slapping and offers to buy the next round. Frank rose to leave as the jukebox began to play "God Rest Ye Merry, Gentlemen." He'd judged the atmosphere at the Mountainside all wrong. Maybe, just for the Christmas season, he should take a page from Joseph's book and be a little more trusting. The sound of the crowd joining in on the refrain followed him into the parking lot, and hung in the still, cold air:

"Oh tidings of comfort and joy, comfort and joy."

As Frank drove past the green on his way home, the floodlights illuminating the Nativity snapped off. In the split second before the brilliance evaporated, Frank thought he noticed something off-kilter. He drove around slowly, waiting for his eyes to adjust to the soft reflection of moonlight on snow. The wooden shepherd offered genuine concern for his shivering lambs. The three kings still marched toward their goal. The donkey's big eyes studied the store and the diner.

When Frank reached the third side of the square, he realized what was wrong.

Joseph was gone.

"What's the point, that's what I'd like to know?"

Unable to sleep most of the night, Frank had rousted Earl out of bed at daybreak and the two of them stood surveying the scene of the Joseph kidnapping. "Bucky made something beautiful for the town and now some idiot has to come along and ruin it." Frank kicked up a cloud of soft snow. "It pisses me off."

"You got any ideas on who coulda done it?"

Frank scowled and shrugged. His favorite usual suspect, Ray Stulke, was both strong enough and stupid enough for the job, but he had the best alibi in town. At the time of the crime, he'd been under Frank's watchful eye at the Mountainside.

"That statue had to weigh 200 pounds," Earl said. "It must've taken them quite a while to haul it out of here."

"They dragged it." Frank looked at the deep parallel gouges the base of the statue had left in the snow. He could only pick out a few intact bootprints; the trampled snow looked as if the thieves had barely lifted their feet as they staggered along with their heavy load. A few deep depressions marked where the thieves had plopped the statue down to take a rest. The trail led to the darkest, least traveled side of the green, where Etta Noakes's house stood in solitary decay.

"We could ask Miss Noakes if she saw anything," Earl suggested. But even as they trudged over to the sagging Victorian, they knew it was hopeless. Miss Noakes was either ninety or ninety-two, depending on how cantankerous she was feeling at the moment you asked her. She opened the door, peering at them through cataract-scarred eyes, and answered their question with the tart reminder that, unlike some people in this town, she did not spend all her time gawping out the window, keeping track of folks coming and going.

She shouted out to them as they left. "It's not someone from town. Bucky Reinholz doesn't have an enemy on this planet. People in Trout Run are damn proud of that Nativity."

Frank hunched his shoulders against the cold, not bothering to acknowledge Etta's remarks. She had a point, but who did that leave? Tourists stashing a 200-pound souvenir in the back of their minivan? Jealous rivals from a town with a mere plaster Nativity? Atheist extremists? Each idea seemed more absurd than the next.

"Maybe it's kids playing a joke," Earl offered hopefully. "Like when the senior class moved the bear from the taxidermy shop to the pulpit of the church."

"That was funny. This..." Frank shook his head. This might be destroying something because the perfection of it cried out for disruption—the freshly painted wall scrawled with graffiti, the windows broken in a row of parked cars. He'd arrested a kid once for shooting out every street light on a block and when he'd asked him why he did it the answer came, "Because I like it dark."

"You want me to drive around and look at places they might've taken it?" Earl asked. "Like maybe the covered bridge, or the cliffs by the river."

Franked snorted. If the statue had been left anywhere obvious they'd have received a dozen calls by now. But Earl was only trying to be helpful. Frank tossed him the patrol car keys. "Yeah, cruise around. See what you turn up." He watched Earl drive off, more worried the kid would find the statue—tossed in a ditch, its head chopped off, or covered in spray paint—than that he wouldn't. He clenched his fists. This was the kind of dread cops felt when a child went missing, when solving the case was often worse than not solving it.

Ridiculous—Joseph was a statue, just a block of wood. A block of wood.

Twenty-four hours and Joseph still hadn't been spotted. The prank theory looked less and less likely--stunts were only fun if everyone could see how clever you'd been. Frank had ended up in the church office on his rounds—futile so far—of looking for a motive for this crime.

"I don't see why you're spending so much time worrying about it," Myrna said. "Since that TV station in Plattsburgh put the theft on the news, more people than ever are coming to see the Nativity."

"Yes, but they're coming for the wrong reason." Bob rolled the new issue of *Presbyterian Life* into a tight cone as he looked out the window at the crowd on the green. "Bucky carved those statues to tell the Christmas story. But the whole story's not there. Now people are coming to see what happened, like rubber-neckers at a car wreck."

"Right reason, wrong reason," Myrna muttered, slapping stamps on the outgoing mail. "Can't you just move one of the shepherds into the manger and call him Joseph?"

Bob spun around behind Myrna's back with the magazine raised high, and for a spilt second Frank felt sure the pastor was going to whack her.

"Sure, put a tricorn hat on Michelangelo's David and call him George Washington." Bob flung his magazine into Myrna's trash can, which rocked with the force of his shot after the pastor was halfway down the hall.

"Well, look who's off his high horse, now that something that matters to *him* has been stolen. No more of that 'turn the other cheek, what would Jesus do' stuff." Myrna tossed her envelopes in the outgoing mail basket. "Now you don't hear him saying, 'If they stole it, they must *really* need it.'" Myrna delivered a cruelly accurate mimicry of Bob's often otherworldly tone. "Nobody really needs a chainsaw Joseph, do they?"

15

"Do you know there's not a single Christmas carol that mentions Joseph?"

Earl looked up from typing a report and frowned at his boss.

"Every figure in the Nativity gets sung about—Mary and Jesus, of course, but the wise men, the shepherds, even the damn cow gets a mention in "Away in a Manger". But not Joseph. No one sings about Joseph."

"And your point is—?"

"My point is, if you were going to steal a statue from a Nativity scene to make some sort of statement, why would you pick that one?" Frank couldn't quite let go of the idea that the Joseph statue had been stolen for a reason. "Why not take Jesus?"

"Too heavy. The baby and the manger are all one piece, carved from that elm stump."

"All right, why not Mary, or a wise man?"

Earl shrugged and answered the ringing phone, leaving Frank to pace the office.

After a few disinterested "all right, okay, uhm-hmms," Earl hung up. "That was Rod Fortney out at the Round Top Mountain Cabins. Says he's got a customer who owes him money. Wants us to go out there."

"What are we, a collection agency? Tell him to buy a vacuum cleaner and some Comet and people might be willing to settle up."

"You want me to go?" Earl asked.

"No," Frank grumbled. "I'll do it. Take my mind off this damn statue."

Any woman who mistakenly crossed the threshold of these cabins took one look at the rust-stained sinks and gray sheets and turned tail, leaving the Round Top as the exclusive domain of young men for whom skiing or fishing or ice-climbing was a flimsy excuse for a weekend of non-stop drinking. Frank was sure he'd find a group of hungover frat boys turning their pockets inside out in a futile search for cash after being informed that the American Express card wasn't welcome here.

But when he arrived the parking lot was empty and Rod stood outside the office, practically hopping up and down.

"Guys skipped out on you?" Frank asked.

"No, they paid for their room. Slipped a check under the door early this morning. Then they sped outta here in that big SUV before I could do my inspection. C'mere." Rod sunk his bony fingers into Frank's arm and pulled him toward the cabins. "See what they done to this room."

The door to cabin seven stood open, allowing the fetid smell of spilled beer, unwashed socks and vomit to waft out. The cramped, four-bed room was certainly filthy, but Frank suspected it hadn't been all that much cleaner when the party checked in.

"I'm goin' to hafta hire the girl to come in and help me clean this. And lookit that big scratch on the paneling." Rod nudged him through the doorway and pointed out a fresh mar in the well-seasoned knotty pine. "And, they stole one of the quilts. There was a matched set in here."

That must make cabin seven the Presidential Suite. Amidst the tangled and strewn bedding there seemed to be only three revolting green and gold quilted bedspreads. So, the charges were really stacking up against these guys: theft of services for precipitating the need for a cleaning lady, plus burglary for one stolen Vietnam War-era bedcover.

"I'll see what I can do, Rod. Can you describe the guys?"

"Big guys, all of 'em. Early twenties. Short hair, and neat clothes, but one of 'em had a big tattoo on his arm. Some kinda snake or lizard or somethin'."

Frank stepped back outside, glad of the crisp air. A patch of color in the black and white landscape caught his eye: a ragged square of green and gold fabric caught on the bare branches of a bush. Beside it were two parallel marks in the snow, as if something had been dragged into the trees behind the cabin. Frank followed the trail until it ended in a small clump of woods. There was a wide depression in the snow, where something heavy and long had clearly been dropped.

"That cloth's from my bedspread." Rod said. "Why'd they bring it out here in the snow?"

Frank continued to stare at the drag marks. "They wrapped something in it. They left it out here over night—there wasn't enough room for it in the cabin. Then they put it in their SUV and drove off with it."

"What was it? Why?"

"I'm pretty sure what, but I can't imagine why."

Frank pulled up in front of 120 Center Street, Glens Falls, the address printed on the check presented by one Russell Begley to pay for cabin seven. Stupid crooks made police work so much easier. And there was the black Ford Expedition, meaning Mr. Begley was home. Frank peered into the back of the huge SUV to see if the Joseph statue was still there, but his luck wasn't running quite that good. The cargo area was empty.

Frank leaned on the bell and the door was soon opened by a tall, well-built young man with an affable face. Was that a shadow of unease when he saw a uniformed cop on his doorstep? If so, he rebounded quickly.

"Good afternoon, officer—what can I do for you?"

"Russell Begley?"

"That's me," he smiled.

"Mr. Begley, you and your friends stayed at the Round Top Mountain Cabins in Trout Run recently, is that so?"

"Uh...yeah."

"You left the room a bit of a mess. Took off with something that didn't belong to you."

Begley looked edgy.

"A green and gold bedspread."

"Oh, yeah, right." The tension drained out of his face. "Look, I'm sorry about that. My friend, he had a little too much to drink, and well, I don't think you'd really want it back now." He reached for his wallet. "I'm happy to pay for it, and any other damage we caused."

"That's very cooperative of you, Mr. Begley." Frank smiled, but made no move to take the proffered money. "I'm also interested in knowing the whereabouts of what you had rolled up in the bedspread."

A fine sheen of sweat broke out on Begley's forehead, and Frank knew he had his man. "In?" the word came out like a cricket's chirp. He cleared his throat and tried again. "Nothing was in the blanket."

"Oh, I think there was. You dragged it behind the cabin, then loaded it into your SUV."

Begley was looking like he might toss his lunch right there. "I don't want to talk to you anymore. I want to call a lawyer."

What a chump! Call in a lawyer for a stupid prank like this. It'd be Easter before they got the statue back if some shyster got in the middle of the process. "Look Mr. Begley, I'm not interested in prosecuting you for this stunt. I want the statue back. As long as it's not damaged, you have nothing to worry about. Give it back to me and I'll leave."

Begley's breathing was audible. Finally he spoke. "The statue. Right. The statue that's been on the news. Well, see, I don't exactly have that anymore."

"Where is it?"

"We, uh, sold it."

"Sold it! To whom?"

"To, uh, a guy. A guy at the rest stop on the Thruway." Begley's words came faster and faster. "He saw it in the SUV and he liked it and asked what did we want for it so he gave us a hundred bucks and we gave him the statue. Because, see, we really didn't want to keep it anymore, after we sobered up." Begley pulled out his wallet again. "Here, you can have that money too."

The next week Begley appeared in municipal court to answer the charge of criminal trespass, pleaded guilty and got probation as a first-time offender. No one went to Attica for stealing chainsaw art. As far as the law was concerned, the case was closed.

As far as Trout Run was concerned, it was wide open.

"Why can't you get this guy to tell you what he did with Joseph?"

That was the question Frank answered all day long, from Bucky and Bob and Earl to people standing in line with him at the Post Office. Over and over he explained that real life wasn't the same as TV, that he didn't get to knock suspects around until they were reduced to quivering wrecks who told all. Not that he wouldn't have liked to rattle the chain of a guy who brought a three-hundred-dollar- an- hour Albany lawyer to a municipal court appearance. Something hinky there.

After a particularly grueling session that ruined his lunch at the diner, Frank headed across the green for the relative safety of his office. He stepped on the path that led through the Nativity scene in time to see a lanky boy shoot out of the church, an aqua Tupperware container clutched under his arm like a football. And there, pursuing him like a Jets linebacker, was Myrna.

"Stop, thief!" Myrna shrieked. "Stop him."

Frank stepped forward to intercept the boy, who dodged him, slipped, and fell in the snow, the Tupperware rolling to a stop in front of a winded Myrna.

"What's going on?" Frank asked, holding the elbow of the squirming boy.

"He stole the chicken salad for the Parish Sages luncheon, that's what's going on," Myrna said. "I was up late last night making that, and he thinks he can stroll off with it. Well, I've had enough! This has got to stop."

By this time Pastor Bob had showed up. "Take your chicken salad and go, Myrna. There's no need to create a scene." He turned to Frank. "Let the boy go."

Frank released the boy's arm and he took off like a rocket. "I think it's time you tell me about your theft problem over there."

"It's Greg Haney's kids." Bob had run out without his coat and stood shivering as he explained. "They're obviously not getting enough to eat at home with their mother dead and their dad disabled, so they've been stealing food from the church. I've called Greg several times offering to help, even went over there, but his daughter insists they're all right. Greg won't even talk to me. He's stubborn and proud."

Frank steered Bob toward his office. Neither of them was eager to encounter Myrna right now. "We'll have to call Social Services."

Bob sighed. "I guess. I hate to get a government bureaucracy involved. We can take care of our own here. Ardyth Munger's been leaving a bag of groceries on the Haneys' porch every week. She sees Greg in his workroom, but he ignores her knocking."

"Well, obviously that's not enough," Frank said as they entered the office. "The county social worker will know how to help."

As Frank worked his way through the department of social services' automated answering system, he glanced at the papers that had landed in his box while he was out. The state police weekly missing persons report.

"Your call is important to us. Please stay on the line," a computerized voice droned in his ear.

He glanced through the report as he waited. A teenage girl in Buffalo, an Alzheimer's patient in Schenectady. Nothing of interest to him.

"All lines are still busy. Please continue to hold."

Frank flipped to the second page of the report. A 23-year old man last seen a week ago in the vicinity of Lake Placid. Travis Monteith. He read with more attention. "Colleagues report Monteith planned to go skiing for the weekend. He never returned to work. Height: 6' 2"; weight: 190; hair: brown, eyes: brown, identifying marks: tattoo of iguana on right forearm."

"Department of Social Services. How may I help you? Hello?"

Frank hung up the phone and grabbed his jacket.

"Where are you going?"

He brushed past Bob. Humiliation at what he had overlooked and dread of what he would find took away his voice.

"Frank, should I come with you?"

"It's too late for that."

Frank pounded on the door of the Haneys' house in the late afternoon twilight. "Police. Open up." To the right of the porch, a one-story wing extended from the house. A soft light glowed behind the sheer curtain of the front window, where a man sat with his head bent. Greg Haney's workroom, but Greg didn't flinch at the racket coming from his front door.

"Danielle Haney, are you in there?" Frank shouted. "Open this door or I'll kick it in."

Frank heard shuffling on the other side of the door, as if the girl had been inches away all along. The door swung inward and Frank saw a tall, slender teenager trembling in the hall. He pushed past her and turned right, into the large rectangular room where Greg Haney repaired guns. Low shelves lined the walls, filled with parts and tools easily within reach of a man confined to a wheelchair. At the worktable by the window a man sat, his head bowed, his forehead furrowed, for all the world concentrating on the disassembled gun before him.

But the work never progressed. The man was made of wood.

Frank turned to find Danielle and her brother, a big, slack-jawed boy, watching him.

"Where is your father?"

"That's a secret!" the boy protested. "Don't tell the man the secret, Danielle, remember?"

The girl looked much smaller to Frank than she had a few minutes before, diminished by weariness and sorrow and fear. She pointed her brother toward the door. "Let's go in the kitchen, Derek. I'll make you hot chocolate." Then she glanced back over her shoulder and nodded slightly in the direction of the back yard. "We had to," she whispered.

Had to. Had to conceal their father's death because they hadn't called a doctor for him when he needed one? Had to let him die because the burden of caring for him had grown too heavy? And he and Bob and Ardyth and Greg's customers had allowed it happen; had kept a safe distance, not wanting to trample on Greg's dignity. The North Country credo—don't butt in.

Frank's fingers felt thick and clumsy as he dialed the state police. The dispatcher kept questioning his requests. Yes, he really did need two crime scene teams. Yes, the second one was to go to the Round Top to look for evidence that Travis Monteith's weekend of drunken partying had taken a nasty turn in cabin seven. He couldn't blame her—she was probably incredulous that any cop could be stupid enough to see evidence of a 200-pound corpse dragged through the snow and mistake it for the signs of a kidnapped statue.

Frank hung up and put his hand on Joseph's shoulder.

He had the statue back, safe and sound. But where was the joy?

Frank watched the choir, clad in down jackets instead of robes, file out of the church and onto the green for the Christmas Eve carol sing. He had a good view of the Nativity. The tourists had all gone home; this event was for Trout Run only. Earl and his girlfriend of the moment held hands. Bucky Reinholz beamed. The Haney kids stood together right up front, Derek in the middle, sheltered by the others.

"Doesn't it make you happy to see those kids together?" Ardyth appeared at his side. "After all Danielle went through to keep them out of foster care."

"You and Bob did a great thing, agreeing to help Danielle so that Social Services would let them keep living together at their house."

"You can share in the credit, Frank. Somehow you made those social workers believe that not reporting Greg's heart attack was perfectly rational."

"Maybe not rational, but not crazy." Frank caught sight of Myrna, almost unrecognizable with a smile on her face. He thought again of what she'd said three weeks before in the church office: "No one really needs a chainsaw Joseph." He'd agreed with her at the time, and now, happily, he understood they'd both been entirely wrong. The Haney kids had had another outlandish task for Joseph and he, no stranger to extraordinary requests, had accepted it.

And now Joseph was back with his family. Frank knew he was being sentimental but he thought Mary looked relieved, grateful that her protector had returned.

The choir began to sing, running through all the old standards: *Joy to the World, Hark the Herald Angels, We Three Kings.* Frank hunched his shoulders as the wind picked up. He'd listen to one or two more, then head home.

Away in a Manger, Silent Night. Frank turned toward his truck as Bob's voice rang out over the green.

"We have one more carol that the choir has learned especially for tonight's performance. It's a German carol from the 14th Century, not very often performed anymore."

Frank smiled and kept walking. The choir director must've been thrilled when Bob came up with this one. And then the music stopped him, the words flowing across the green and carried by the breeze into the starry night:

"Joseph Dearest, Joseph Mine,

Help me cradle the child divine;

God reward thee and All that's thine

In paradise,"

So prays the mother Mary.

LOSERS WEEPERS

When Trout Run Municipal Park Clean-Up Day rolled around, Ardyth Munger knew better than to arrive late.

Last year she had stopped at Malone's Diner for breakfast—never a quick affair—and by the time she got to the park the only assignment left was cleaning behind the rest rooms, a part of the park that saw all its activity after the sun went down. This year, when Police Chief Frank Bennett arrived at 8:45 to coordinate the day's activities, Ardyth was already sitting in the parking lot, work gloves in hand, ready for her assignment.

"How about cleaning the toddler playground?" Frank suggested. Still lean and spry at seventy-two, Ardyth strongly resisted efforts to shunt her off to little old lady activities. But Frank knew she'd rather collect chewed up old pacifiers than empty beer bottles, Skoal tins, and butts that even Ardyth knew didn't contain tobacco.

"If that's where you need me," she said and marched off.

29

Although the weather had been uncommonly balmy for an Adirondack May, only a fool or a tourist would believe spring was here to stay. With snow showers predicted later in the week, Frank was anxious to get all the park improvement projects finished. Engrossed in unclogging the water fountain, he didn't notice Ardyth's return.

"Look what I found, Frank." She dangled something shiny in her hand. "A gold locket."

He reached for a wrench. "Finders keepers. Lucky you."

"No, Frank—I can't keep it. This is valuable."

She pushed the necklace under his nose. The clasp on the delicate gold chain had caught on something and snapped.

"Feel how heavy and satiny the locket is. I'm sure this is eighteen-carat gold." Ardyth examined the intricate filigree design of the case. "This is an heirloom. We have to find the person who lost it."

Frank sat back on his heels and stared at her.

"Oh, relax. I didn't mean you had to launch an investigation. Just keep it at the police department and I'll put a lost and found ad in the *Mountain Herald*."

"Take that up with Doris." The town secretary maintained a huge lost and found box behind her desk into which a stream of single mittens, reading glasses, umbrellas, and sneakers thrown out the school bus window made their way. So far as Frank knew, no one had ever claimed anything although occasionally people trapped by a sudden Adirondack rainstorm came in and borrowed one of the umbrellas.

"No, it can't go in the box with all that junk. It would be safest with you."

Frank sighed and held out his hand. As Ardyth dropped the locket in his palm, he noticed the tiny hinge. "Why don't you open it? If there's a picture inside, maybe we can figure out who it belongs to."

"Of course—how silly of me." Ardyth popped the locket open.

Inside was a black and white photo, maybe an inch and a quarter long. A young man, cocky and grinning, stood with his arm around the shoulders of a slender woman. He wore a military uniform, she a dress with a cinched waist and a wide, white collar.

Ardyth tilted the locket into the sunlight. "From the hairstyles and the clothes, I'd say this was taken in the Fifties. His face is clearer than hers. She must have moved right when the camera snapped. There's something about them...but no, I can't tell who they are. "Can you?"

Frank squinted for a better look although if a life-long Trout Runner like Ardyth didn't recognize the couple, he surely wouldn't. The picture was tiny and faded, but one thing was clear. The two were in love.

Frank pulled the patrol car into the town office parking lot and dragged himself out of the vehicle. Keeping the men with chainsaws apart from the middle-schoolers with rakes was more exhausting than digging a ten-foot trench. Next year, he'd put Earl in charge of Clean-Up Day.

As if on cue, Earl came charging out the office door, drawing up short at the sight of his boss. "Wow, what timing! I thought I was going to have to go out on this call alone."

Frank detected a note of disappointment. There was a time when he wouldn't have let his civilian assistant handle a stray dog call on his own, but the kid had come a long way in two years. Earl was studying at the Police Academy now, and by next year he'd been sworn in as an officer. As long as this call wasn't dangerous, Frank was happy to let Earl take it.

"Roy Corvin's been shot!" Earl practically bounced with excitement. He hadn't quite mastered a cop's unflappable detachment.

"Hunting accident?"

Earl pulled a face. "Roy Corvin's no hunter. More likely he pissed someone off."

Frank got back in the patrol car, waiting for Earl to buckle in before flipping on the siren and peeling out of the lot. "Which way?"

"Roy rents that little house behind Bill McKenna's machine shop out on Ridge Road." Earl was a human MapQuest for Trout Run, able to provide not only addresses and directions for every home in town, but also complete background information on every resident.

"Roy Corvin was way ahead of me in school," he continued. "But he never graduated. Dropped out and couldn't hold a job. Finally he joined the Army, but he was back home in four months. Claimed he had bad hearing in one ear, but I bet he got thrown out."

"The Army needs every warm body they can get these days. They're willing to overlook quite a few problems."

"Army didn't even want Roy for defusing roadside bombs. That says a lot."

Frank took his eyes off the road for a moment to look at his assistant. It wasn't like Earl to be so negative. This must be personal.

"What'd Roy Corvin ever do to you?"

Earl turned his head toward the window. Gazing at Whiteface shrouded in clouds, or Stony Brook winding through a stand of white birch could be irresistible, even to a native, but at this particular moment they were passing Al's Sunoco.

"Earl?"

"My cousin Ruthann dated him for a while. Got taken in by his looks. Let's just say it wasn't a happy time for anyone in the family."

"Abusive?"

"First Ruthann stopped coming to family parties. Then my Uncle Dave spotted her at the supermarket with a black eye. A couple of us paid Roy a little visit. Now Ruthann is engaged to a schoolteacher from Saranac Lake."

Frank slapped the edge of the steering wheel. "Earl, I'm warning you, when you become a sworn law enforcement officer, you can't take part in these family vengeance operations. 'Protect and Serve' is our motto, not 'Judge and Punish.' Roy is the victim here." Frank pulled up beside an ambulance parked in front of Roy Corvin's house. "Keep an open mind."

Two members of the rescue squad carried a stretcher toward them. A young man, his face starkly pale against his dark hair and red-soaked shirt, lay limp as the third member of the team labored over him. "Looks like the bullet collapsed his right lung," the paramedic said. "He's in shock--lost a lot of blood. We have to get on the road."

The ambulance took off as Frank and Earl turned toward the house. Bill from the machine shop waited for them on the porch. He didn't need questions to get him talking.

"I was working on a lawnmower engine when I thought I heard a shot. Then I heard a car tearing out. By the time I got outside, the car was over the crest of the hill. Roy didn't answer the door, so I went in." He paused for a breath. "Roy was layin' on the kitchen floor, a hole in his chest. I called you guys ad did what

I could to help him." He looked down at his hands, back with grease and red with blood.

"Did he say who did it?" Frank asked.

"His lips moved a little, then he passed out." Bill shook his head. "I don't know 'bout Roy. For a while he was working regular over at the lumberyard, but lately he's been home all day and out all night. Two months behind on his rent. Now this."

Frank thanked Bill and sent him on his way before he and Earl entered the house. Passing through the beer can-strewn living room, they stopped at the door to the kitchen. Blood had pooled in a low spot on the cracked linoleum floor. A chair lay on its side, drawers and cabinets hung open, papers and food wrappers covered every level surface. It was hard to tell if the place had been ransacked or if this was the usual state of Roy's housekeeping. Frank picked his way carefully through the mess, his eye drawn by a spot of orange plastic on the table.

A prescription pill bottle, empty. He used the tip of a pencil to roll it over and read the label aloud. "OxyContin."

"That's a powerful narcotic," Earl volunteered, having recently aced an exam on drugs of abuse.

"Prescribed for a Marcus Philhower," Frank said.

"We prayed for him in church last week. He's got liver cancer."

Frank sighed. "Nice. Roy stole a dying man's painkillers, then someone popped him to steal them again."

Earl did not say "I told you so." Didn't even smirk. More and more these days, Frank thought the kid had the makings of a damn good cop.

Earl hung up the phone and spun around on his desk chair as Frank returned from canvassing Corvin's neighbors. "Mrs. Philhower didn't even notice the OxyContin was gone. Her husband's on morphine now."

"Interesting," Frank said. "I wonder if Roy knew the drugs wouldn't be missed?"

"Mrs. Philhower says she doesn't know Roy. She was a little freaked out thinking that he came right into her husband's room to steal the stuff."

"I suppose she leaves her doors unlocked like everyone else in trout Run." Frank stuck his hands in his pockets and jingled his change, pacing the office as he thought aloud. "Roy could have taken the drugs himself, but maybe he had an accomplice. I don't suppose you know which unlucky lady took your cousin's place in Roy's affections?"

"No, but I can ask the bartenders at the Mountainside. Roy's a regular."

"Good. The hospital will call us when Roy's able to talk. No one on Ridge Road saw or heard anything. What about Roy's parents?"

"His dad was killed in a motorcycle accident when he was a baby, then his mom ran off with another guy and left him with his grandparents, Deke and Connie Steuben."

Frank looked up a number, reached for the phone, and dialed. After a moment he announced, "No answer. They're probably over at the hospital with Roy."

Frank's brow wrinkled as his fingers touched something unfamiliar in his pocket. He pulled out the locket. "Here's another mystery for you, Earl. Do you recognize these people?"

Earl studied the picture. "Don't know the guy. There's something kinda familiar about the woman, but her face is blurry. Where'd you get it?"

Frank explained Ardyth's discovery. "She wants me to keep it here while she runs a lost-and-found ad in the *Herald*. I'd better tell Doris, in case someone really does call."

Frank took the locket to the secretary's desk in the outer office. Doris immediately put aside her filing for this far more interesting project.

"Hmmm. I don't recognize them, but the guy's awful handsome." She ran her rough fingers over the gold wistfully. "This sure is beautiful. Expensive too. Ardyth is right—I can't throw it in the lost and found box."

Frank peered into the overflowing bin behind her desk. "Why don't you get rid of some of that stuff, Doris? Face it—tourists who left their gloves here during the '80 Winter Olympics aren't coming back for them."

"None of it's that old, Frank. Why, I didn't even start the lost and found until '86...or was it '88?"

"Doris," Frank warned.

"All right, I guess I could give some of the stuff on the bottom to the church clothing bank."

"Great idea." Frank returned to his office and left her to her new assignment. Half an hour later, Doris appeared in front of him, a loaded shopping bag in one hand and a little yellow rain slicker printed with green frogs in the other.

"I'm going to take this bag over to the church now," Doris said, "But I was wondering about this coat. It's Hanna Anderson..."

"So if you know it belongs to Hanna, call her mom to come get it." Why Doris needed him to authorize the simplest phone call was beyond Frank.

"No, no—Hanna Anderson is the designer who makes it. Her stuff is so cute, but it's awful expensive." She stopped and looked at the coat longingly.

Frank took a deep breath. "What are you getting at, Doris?"

"I was just wondering...well..." She spit the rest out in a rush, "if you thought it would be okay to give this coat to my granddaughter, Julie."

"Sure. Go ahead."

"Really? Because I don't want to do anything dishonest. Maybe I should wait another year."

Do not yell. Do not yell. She can't help herself. "Give it to her now, Doris. She's not going to want it when she goes off to college."

"Oh, Frank! You're such a card. You make me laugh all the time."

Frank massaged his temples. "Yeah, same here."

"I hope we have better luck finding the owner of that locket." Doris pointed to the puddle of gold on Frank's desk blotter. "You'd better not leave it lying around."

He pulled his keys from his pocket and looked at Earl and Doris. "Remember, if someone actually comes to claim the necklace, they have to describe it to get it. I'm locking it up in my top desk drawer, right in the petty cash box."

"Roy Corvin's taken a turn for the worse," Frank reported as Earl came into the office the next morning. "He picked up an infection in his good lung. He's on a respirator, under heavy sedation."

"That's one way to get your drugs." Earl handed Frank a cup of coffee, a sweet roll, a quarter and a dime. "They were out of jelly donuts so I had to get you a Danish. That's why your change is only thirty-five cents."

"Good choice. Did you get to the Mountainside last night?"

"Yeah, I took Molly over there for a drink, and—"

"Molly? Molly Lynch?" Frank whistled. Molly was a cute little college girl who wouldn't have given Earl a second glance a few months ago. "Man, you're a regular babe magnet since you enrolled in the Police Academy. Just wait until you get your badge and gun."

Earl's grin teetered between shy and smug. "So anyway, the bartender says Roy was hooked up with Tiffany Kass. Guess what she does for a living?"

"Cleaning lady? Home health aide?"

Earl shot a rubber band at his boss. "Bingo. I stopped in at the Philhowers' this morning. Tiffany's been working there three days a week for the past month. Mrs. P says she wasn't crazy about her, but she needed the help."

"Outstanding, Earl." Frank downed the last sugary bite of his breakfast. There was a time when Earl wouldn't have shown the initiative to substitute a Danish for a donut. Now he was following up on leads and asking all the right questions. "Let's go pay a call on this little angel of mercy. If Roy dies, we've got a murder investigation on our hands."

Tiffany Kass lived with her mother and sister and a passel of kids of various ages. The house slumped as if one good Adirondack snowstorm would flatten it, but since it was still standing in May, Frank figured it was good for another six months. Tiffany herself was not bad looking, if you could get past the dark roots and unicorn tattoo. She sat at her sticky kitchen table radiating resentment.

"I don't know nuthin' about it."

"Let me refresh your memory," Frank said. "You were working as a home health aide for the Philhowers. You took a prescription bottle of OxyContin from the nightstand in Mr. Philhower's bedroom and gave it to your boyfriend, Roy Corvin. That's a felony."

Tiffany picked at a crusty clot of dried breakfast cereal. "You can't prove that."

Frank leaned across the table, forcing eye contact. "You know what, Tiffany? I don't have to prove it. All I have to do is tell your probation officer you've been associating with a known drug user." Frank shot a look at a T-shirt clad toddler waddling by with a sodden diaper drooping nearly to her knees. "And the child welfare department might be interested in hearing about it too."

Tiffany tapped into a hidden reserve of energy. "You leave that bitch social worker out of this! I'm not losing my kids 'cause a Roy Corvin."

"Then talk. I know you were in Elizabethtown meeting with your probation officer at the time Roy was shot. Who else knew he had those drugs?"

Tiffany shrugged. "There was only a few left in the bottle. Roy wasn't about to share them."

"How about selling them? Does he have regular customers?"

Tiffany shook her head. "Roy's not into dealing. You gotta be able to collect enough from everyone to pay your supplier. Roy got messed up with that once. He don't do it no more."

"So who had a beef with Roy? Who could have shot him?"

"Roy's had fights with half the guys at the Mountainside. And he's screwed half the girls. Go talk to them about it."

Tiffany rose and took a sudden interest in cleaning the kitchen. Frank thought the clatter of dishes flung into the sink very effectively masked her sniffling. "Was there another woman, Tiffany?" he asked gently.

"Some chick I don't know. He'd sit around waiting for her to call." Tiffany snorted. "Not that he could've been doing much with her, loaded up on painkillers like he was. I shoulda stolen him some Viagra."

The toddler reappeared and wrapped her arms around her mother's leg. Tiffany scooped her up. "I really don't care who shot him. I'm done with Roy Corvin."

"What do you think?" Frank asked Earl when they were back in the patrol car. "Does Roy really not have enough ambition to sell pills?"

"I think Tiffany's right—you have to be able to manage accounts to have regular customers. But that doesn't mean Roy wouldn't sell a pill or two to another druggie."

"I think I'll pay a visit to the Moutainside tonight," Frank said. "In the meantime, let's call on the grandparents."

The Steubens' house wasn't any bigger than Tiffany's, bit it was light years apart in atmosphere. Cheerful clumps of daffodils lined the walk, a U.S. flag snapped smartly in the breeze, and a "Welcome Friends" plaque hung over a woodpecker-shaped door knocker. Before Frank could bang the beak, the door opened.

"Saw you coming." Deke Steuben, still powerfully built although well into retirement, ushered them into the immaculate living room. "Have a seat." He pointed Frank and Earl toward the floral sofa draped with a zigzag afghan. "I suppose this is about Roy."

"Yes." Frank glanced around. "Is your wife home too?"

"Nah, Connie's still at the hospital." Deke ran a big paw over his silver crew cut. "I couldn't take it anymore. I had to come home."

"I'm sorry for your trouble, Deke. We're working hard to find out who did this."

Deke looked away, his eyes blinking hard. "What difference does it make? Roy's always mixed up with the wrong kind of people. You lock this one up, someone else will come along to take his place."

Frank exchanged a glance with Earl. You might expect that kind of despair from a resident of a housing project in the Bronx, but it wasn't typical in Trout Run. "We're hoping you can tell us about Roy's friends, men and women. Especially if there are any you know who are drug users."

Deke snorted. "I imagine all of them are. I don't want to know his so-called friends or the sluts he sleeps with. Last winter we sent Roy to one of those clinics where they get you off the drugs. It cost a fortune. But it seemed like money well spent because he came back here and got a job and everything was great. Didn't last, though. By March it all started again—the late night calls begging Connie for money, the lumberyard calling here when Roy didn't show up for work."

Deke nodded toward a cabinet in the corner. "He even stole one of my guns. That was the last straw. I changed the locks on the doors, and now I keep this place bolted up like we live in goddam Detroit. I told Connie we're not giving him one more penny, I don't care if he's starving."

They sat in silence for a moment. But Deke wasn't done. He seemed relieved to abandon his North Country stoicism. Frank and Earl already knew the worst, so why not share everything? "You see that picture?" Deke pointed to a wall covered with framed photos interspersed with mounted deer antlers. Near the center was a picture of a little boy in a bow tie holding a trumpet. "That's Roy in fifth grade when he had a solo with the school band and won a prize. I swear that's the last time he ever did anything we could be proud of."

Deke shook his head. "Right after that was when our daughter Theresa, Roy's mother, disappeared for good. She left Roy with us and she never came back."

"Did you try to track her down?" Frank asked.

"Oh, yeah—for years. But it was too hard on Connie and Roy. Finally I said we just had to put it behind us. That's why Connie's always been soft on Roy, making excuses for him. She feels like she failed with Theresa. But none of the others turned out bad." He gestured back to the wall, where young women in graduation gowns and wedding gowns beamed. "We have two other daughters, Nancy and Karen. They're great girls, married nice fellas, had kids who all went to college and got good jobs. Only Roy. Only Roy has these terrible problems."

Deke leaned back in his recliner, his eyes still focused on the wall of photos, his mind somewhere far in the past. Frank could see he would be of no further use to them. He rose to go, nudging Earl, who also sat staring at the wall.

"You take care, Deke. We'll keep you posted on what we find."

Deke struggled to get up from his chair, his hands trembling. "Whatever it is, it won't be good."

"You're awfully quiet, " Frank said after they had driven halfway back to the office without Earl saying a word.

"I'm thinking maybe I've been a little hard on Roy. Imagine your mom dropping you off for a weekend with your grandparents, then never coming back. And having aunts like Nancy and Karen who are nice, normal moms and yours doesn't give a damn. No wonder Roy's screwed up."

"Seems like his grandfather's given up on him," Frank said.

"But not his grandma. Maybe if Roy recovers from this gunshot, he'll finally be able to turn himself around."

"Possibly," Frank said. Earl's eternal optimism was one of his most endearing qualities and Frank had to remind himself not to shoot it down. Maybe this was the rock-bottom Roy had to hit in order to bounce back. Or maybe it was one more stop on the long downward spiral.

"Why were you so interested in Deke's family photos?" Frank asked, to change the subject. "Do you know all those kids?"

"Not really," Earl said. "I've never been to the Steubens' house, but I had a feeling I'd seen some of the photos before. Weird. Like, whattayacallit?"

"Déjà vu."

Frank spent two hours that night in the Mountainside Tavern, talking to Roy Corvin's known associates, but all he got for his trouble was a raw throat from breathing in secondhand smoke and a pounding headache from trying to hear over the blare of the jukebox. Roy's cronies, reluctant to speak ill of the almost dead, had to be prodded to talk, but the general consensus was that since Roy had fallen off the rehab wagon, he was irritable and unstable, and everyone had been avoiding him.

Not that Frank expected anyone to own up to visiting Roy on the afternoon in question. But by getting each man propped at the bar to identify someone else as being a better friend of Roy, he'd managed to compose a list of people whose whereabouts at the time of the shooting would have to be checked. But no one knew anything about another girlfriend.

Frank stopped back at the office to write up his interview notes while they were fresh in his mind. The fluorescent tube above his computer flickered maddeningly. He stood on his desk and jiggled it. The bulb settled into a steady glow. He sat back down and continued typing. Immediately, the light pulsed dim and bright and commenced a high-pitched hum. He typed a few more lines and decided to call it quits.

Hopping back up onto the desk, Frank yanked out the tube. Might as well stop by the hardware store on the way in tomorrow, he thought. And better take ten bucks from petty cash now, otherwise he'd forget to reimburse himself.

Frank unlocked the top desk drawer. Inside the olive green metal petty cash box was $23.74. He took a ten and shut the drawer.

Then he opened it again. $23.74. That's all.

No gold locket.

After a restless night puzzling over the missing locket, Frank went directly to the Trout Run Presbyterian Church for consultation with his friend, Pastor Bob Rush. He paced around the minister's book-crammed office, laying out the details of the problem as much for his own benefit as for Bob's.

"And the only people who know where I put the locket are Earl, Doris, and Ardyth," Frank concluded.

"But if it was locked in your drawer--?"

"Earl and Doris know where the spare key is, in case they ever have to use the petty cash when I'm out. And Ardyth is the town treasurer. She uses that key when she comes in to replenish the cash and collect the receipts."

"Well, it can't be Ardyth," Bob said. "No one does God's work more faithfully than she does."

Frank might've rolled his eyes if he had heard anyone else described so piously, but in Ardyth's case, Bob was absolutely right. Ardyth was a good person. Not holier than thou, just good and kind, through and through. And not a Pollyanna either. Frank wouldn't have been able to tolerate that. No, Ardyth saw people's flaws clearly enough, but she helped them anyway. She would no sooner sneak into the town office and take that locket than she would rob a bank.

"I know," Frank said. "She made such a big deal about turning it in when she found it, so why steal it back?"

Bob shook his head. "Definitely not Ardyth. So that leaves Doris and Earl."

Frank dropped his head in his hands. "It can't be Doris. She's just too, too..."

"Dumb?" Bob offered helpfully.

"Yeah, but lots of crooks are dumb. Doris is transparent. She's like a cartoon character—I can practically see her thoughts floating in a bubble over her head. If she stole it, she'd give herself away."

The two men sat in silence.

"Earl?" Bob said finally.

Frank squirmed as if spiders were crawling over him. "I can't accept that. His work has improved dramatically. He's doing great at the Academy." Frank shut his eyes. "He's really coming along."

"Yet you have doubts," Bob said.

"Something he mentioned the other day. Apparently he's dating Molly Lynch."

"The dentist's daughter?"

"That's the one. What if he felt the need to impress her? You know – support her in the manner to which she's accustomed."

"A young woman like Molly wouldn't want some quaint old locket," Bob said. "Besides, Earl would be smart enough to know his girlfriend couldn't be seen wearing stolen goods."

Frank sighed. "He'd also be smart enough to know how to fence it. Trade it in for something flashier, or get cash for a night out in Lake Placid."

"Is he that crazy about her?" Bob asked.

"I don't know. Or maybe he needed money for some family emergency. Earl's passionately loyal to his family. But I can't believe he jeopardize his career as a police officer for something so stupid. Not after he worked so hard to get into the Academy."

Frank stood up and crossed to the window. He looked out at the town green, where the crocuses planted by the garden club were bowed down under the weight of the promised spring snow. "I don't give a damn about that stupid necklace. I just hate that three people I like and trust are the only ones who could have taken it."

"Morning, all," Doris chirped.

Frank jumped as she came up behind him, twitchy as a cat at the vet.

"Did I mention I ran into Ardyth the night before last, taking a casserole to Mrs. Philhower? I told her you had the necklace locked up safe and sound."

Frank watch Doris's every gesture, completely keyed into her patter for the first time in their working lives together. He felt like a spy in his own office, a narc for internal affairs. No wonder everyone despised those guys. Was she testing him? Trying to determine if he discovered the loss?

"The ad will be in today's paper. Maybe someone will call." Doris chatted on, as excited and optimistic as a child with a raffle ticket.

"I almost described it to my husband last night, but then I caught myself. I remembered what you said about not spreading around what the locket looks like." She turned an imaginary key in front of her mouth. "Loose lips sink ships!"

Frank could barely stand to watch her. No way Doris knew the necklace was gone. No way she had taken it. He glanced over at Earl.

The kid's fingers flew over the keyboard, his eyes locked on the terminal screen. Was Earl pretending not to hear Doris, or did he have her tuned out, as they both usually did? Doris returned to her desk while Frank a pencil on a pile of papers and listened to the rapid click of the keys. He realized how much he'd come to rely on Earl as a sounding board, testing out ideas, thinking aloud. Keeping this secret felt ridiculously like infidelity.

The locket nonsense was distracting him from the real work of finding out who shot Roy Corvin. He wanted to shove the matter aside and forget about it, but sooner or later Doris would open that drawer and...

Frank's tapping became so agitated that the pencil bounced out of his hand and sailed across the room.

Earl looked up. "What's bugging you?"

"Nothing." Frank replied too quickly. "Here, I made a list of Roy Corvin's friends. You follow up on the first four. See where they were when he was shot."

"No problem." Earl took the list, giving Frank a puzzled look as he went out the door.

Frank sat and stared at the remaining names on the list. Two of them had had some trouble—drunk driving, a domestic disturbance—but that had been a couple of years back. They were good guys, working men—a little rough but basically decent. He would check them out, but he doubted it would lead to anything. Frank reached for the phone. Maybe Bill McKenna would remember something else, now that the shock of discovering Roy's bleeding body had subsided.

Bill tried his best to be helpful, but he had a little new to offer. He hadn't noticed any car other than Tiffany's at Roy's house in the days before the shooting. He hadn't heard the sound of arguing—his shop was too noisy. Roy had never confided his problems.

"I suspected he must have lost his job, but I didn't like to ask," Bill said. "I figured I'd give him one more month on the rent before I made him leave. 'Course the phone company wasn't that generous. They had already cut off his service."

"How do you know?" Frank asked.

"When I found him I tried to call for help from his house, but the line was dead, so I had to run back to my shop. But I got to give our rescue squad credit. They got there awful fast."

Frank's grip on the phone tightened. "Yeah, they sure did."

"Doris!" Frank bellowed for the secretary before the receiver was back in the cradle. "Check the log. What time did Bill McKenna's call reporting Roy's shooting come in?"

"At 4:47."

"And what exactly did you do next?"

"I told Earl, and he headed right out."

Frank nodded. He remembered glancing at the clock is he and Earl had pulled out of the parking lot that afternoon. It had been 4:49. They had arrived at Roy's at 5:02—yet the volunteer rescue squad, which was also coming from the center of Trout Run, was already there working on Roy when he and Earl had showed up.

"Then I called it into Roger from the rescue squad," Doris continued. "But the funny thing is, Roger's wife told me he was already on the way. Someone else must've called him directly."

"Yeah, someone. The shooter."

Roger Einhorn confirmed that the call reporting Roy's injury had come not from Bill McKenna or Doris, but from a woman "screaming hysterically so I could barely understand her."

Frank smiled. The solution to Roy Corvin's shooting required nothing more than a request to the phone company to see whose phone had made the call. In less than half an hour he had the answer.

"Esther Neugeberger?" Frank repeated. "Are you sure?"

"Yes sir, that's who the cellular number is registered to."

Esther, an elderly lady hobbled by arthritis, certainly hadn't made a quick escape from Roy Corvin's house. Ten minutes of rambling, confused conversation with her revealed two salient facts: she hadn't used her cell phone since April, when her car stalled at the supermarket, and she now had some help with her housework. Tiffany Kass.

Frank leaned back in his chair and closed his eyes. He might have known finding Roy's shooter couldn't be that easy. But at least he knew the shooter was a woman, a woman who was upset about what she had done to Roy and didn't want him to die. A woman who grabbed a stolen cell phone at Roy's house and used it to call for help. Frank reached for the phone again. He should call Earl back in—he was on a wild goose chase following up on Roy's male friends. Frank let his fingers slip off the phone. Easier to have Earl away and occupied than to be with him, pretending neither of them knew about the missing locket and what its theft meant to Earl's future in law enforcement.

Tiffany's suspicion that there was another woman in Roy's life seemed increasingly probable, so Frank set out to talk to the one person he had not yet asked about Roy's love life – his grandmother. Talking to Connie Steuben entailed a long drive to the hospital in Plattsburgh, where she was keeping a vigil at her grandson bedside.

Frank felt his lunch curdle in his stomach at the first whiff of hospital air. He could cope with the stink of an autopsy better than this aroma of impending death. The intensive care unit bore uncanny similarities to a maximum-security cell block: bright lights, constant noise, relentless scrutiny. Wire and tubes shackled the patients as effectively as chains. Frank finally spotted a familiar, careworn face: it was Connie Steuben, sitting beside an inert form.

"Hello, Connie. How's it going?"

The question was purely rhetorical. Connie's sunken eyes and stringy hair told the tale of too many nights spent dozing in the hospital hard, leatherette chair.

"Why are you here?" Her face was too haggard to register any further worry.

Frank told her about the hysterical woman's call to the rescue squad. "I think she might be the shooter. Do you have any idea what women he was seeing other than Tiffany?"

Connie shook her head and stroked her grandson's face. Even with the beard grown during his hospitalization and the tube forcing air into his lungs, Roy retained his handsome profile. "He always had girls chasing him, even in kindergarten. But he never stuck with any of them, not even the nice ones. I stopped keeping track. He was always searching, searching for something more. More love to fill up the hole in his heart."

"What about your daughters? Would they know anything?"

Connie fussed with the bedcovers. "The girls don't bother with Roy anymore. Not since the drugs and the stealing. They side with their father."

Frank thought of the family pictures on the Steubens' wall. Karen and Nancy looked like Deke—broad, solid, placid. He imagined them forming an unyielding barrier against their nephew's restless, urgent needs. Or a united front to protect their parents.

Frank placed his hand on the old woman's plump shoulder. "Why don't you let me drive you back to Trout Run? You need a good night's sleep."

Connie shrugged out of his grasp. "No. I can't leave Roy. I'm all he's got."

"What's going on?"

Frank return to the office to find Earl and Doris huddled over the drawer containing the petty cash box.

Doris jumped, so used to being scolded by Frank that she assumed she must've done something wrong.

Earl glanced up from fitting the key in the desk drawer lock. Frank watched the scene unfold with the sense of helpless inevitability he felt when a deer sprang in front of his car. The locket wouldn't be there. The three of them would confront one another. The crash would come.

Frank heard the cashbox click open.

A moment later, the gold locket hung glimmering from Earl's fingers. "I think I may have found the woman whose picture's in the locket," Earl said. "I need to see it again to be sure."

Frank felt words ready to surge out, but he choked them back. Relief at an impossible reprieve washed through him. All this worry for nothing. But at the same time, in a deeper part of his brain, confusion throbbed. Was he getting senile? How could he have overlooked the locket? But no —he'd dumped out the box and searched the entire drawer. Two days ago that locket hadn't been there.

Now Earl was trying to pry the delicate thing open, without success. Doris took it from him and sprang it with her fingernail. Her brow furrowed, her jaw dropped, her eyes saucered—a dead ringer for Olive Oyl.

"It's empty! The picture's gone!"

At least this time, Frank didn't have to bother concealing his shock. He wasn't crazy—the locket had been gone, and now it was back. But he was wrong—wrong about why it had been stolen. Wrong, all wrong, to have suspected Earl. He felt a hot rush of shame race up his neck into his cheeks. He turned his head away, sure that Earl could read every despicable thought it had ever contained.

Doris hadn't stopped babbling. "Who took it? Did you, Frank? Why would someone take just the picture? Who could've got into that drawer? I swear I didn't tell a soul, not a soul."

"Okay, Doris – don't worry about it. A little mix-up. I think I hear someone in the outer office." Frank nudged her out toward her desk, then shut the door and faced Earl.

"What?"

"Remember when we were at the Steubens' house and I said I felt like I'd seen those photos on the wall before?" Earl began. "Well, today I was tracking down Roy's friend Butch Farley, the plumber, and I found him working on a job. And the house where he was working had a whole wall of photos, just like the Steubens, except arranged better, like a timeline. And I saw one of the same photos there as the Steubens have hanging in their house."

"Where? Whose house were you in today?"

"Ardyth Munger's. See, that's why I had déjà vu. Because I've been to Ardyth's house lots of times, and whenever I'm there I like to look at the old pictures on her wall. The town green with horses and buggies going through it, Ardyth's dad on wooden skis. But this picture is from later—right before the photos switch over from black-and-white to color."

"So you're telling me the photo from the locket is also hanging on Ardyth's wall and the Steubens' wall?"

Earl shook his head. "No, I don't think so. That's why I wanted to look at the locket picture again. I think I recognize the woman from the locket, or really, the dress from the locket, because you can't see her face that clearly. The two photos at Ardyth's and

Deke's have a woman in that dress standing next to a man in uniform."

Earl held the necklace up to eye level. "But it's not the man in the locket. It's a different soldier—I'm sure of that."

Frank sneezed. "Have you found it yet?"

"Hold your flashlight steady," Pastor Bob said. The two men were combing through the archives of the Presbyterian Church, hampered by clouds of dust and the dim glow of a 40-watt bulb in the file room ceiling. "I think I'm in the right year. Yes, here it is: July 12, 1952, Constance Fortier married to Deke Steuben.

"Right towards the end of the Korean War," Frank said. "Now, look for Theresa Steuben's baptismal record."

"She was baptized in May of 1953. But she was born in early February."

"Less than nine months from the wedding." Frank moved the beam of his flashlight back to the marriage certificate file. "Hey, does that certificate say who the witnesses were?"

"Yes." Bob rechecked the file. "Witnesses: Ardyth Sampson and George Munger."

Bob tugged at his clerical collar, leaving a distinct black fingerprint on the pristine white. "Is it really necessary to confront Ardyth with this, Frank? She must have been trying to spare her friend more heartache by taking the picture out of the locket before anyone recognized that Connie had saved a memento of her youthful indiscretion."

"She didn't have to sneak in and steal it to do that," Frank said. "She could have come directly to me and I would've given it to her, no questions asked, no reporting to Doris or Earl. Ardyth knows me well enough to be sure of that. No, there's something more going on here."

Bob closed the file drawers and sneezed. "You're too suspicious, Frank. The poor woman took the photo out and put the locket back because she must have realized you'd suspect Doris and Earl. Where's the harm?"

"I told you before, Bob—I don't give a damn about that necklace. But I do care who put Roy Corvin into a coma that he may never come out of. And that broken locket has got something to do with it."

Despite serving Frank tea and gingersnaps in her parlor, Ardyth Munger sat looking at her guest is if she fully expected he would knock her around to get her to talk.

Frank clasped his mug and leaned forward. Ardyth shrank into the chintz. "Ardyth, I'm not mad at you for taking the locket and destroying the picture. But I think there's something you're not telling me. Something to do with Roy's shooting."

"Don't be silly. The locket has nothing to do with that."

Frank reached for another cookie. This might take a while. "Okay, start at the beginning and tell me how you realized the locket was Connie's."

"I can't believe I didn't make the connection to the dress when I opened the locket." She waved at her living room wall where Connie and Deke's wedding pictures still hung. "These have been here so long, I guess I don't see them anymore. If only I had...."

Ardyth twisted a loose thread on her sleeve. "Anyway, last week after Roy was shot, I drove up to the hospital. I made Connie come with me to the coffee shop for a snack. To distract her from her troubles, I told her about finding the locket. Well, I thought the poor woman was having a stroke! When she finally got hold of herself, she told me some things I never knew.

"You see, Connie and Deke got engaged before Deke shipped out to Korea," Ardyth continued. "She was only seventeen —a beautiful girl, full of fun. A group of us used to go up to this dance hall in Plattsburgh, near the Air Force base. Connie couldn't stand to sit home, so she'd come along and dance with the airmen. That's where she met the other fellow."

Ardyth brushed some cookie crumbs into her napkin. "She and Deke got married when he came home on leave—a small wedding." She looked up. "Connie loved Deke, Frank, she did. I don't think she even knew she was, was—"

"Already pregnant with the other guy's baby."

Ardyth choked on her tea but kept talking. "So Theresa was born a little premature and Deke came home and everything was fine. Then Nancy and Karen came along. And people always commented how different Theresa was from the other girls. Slender and dark and quick as a whippet. And wild. She always had a bunch of boyfriends, and she fought with Deke about them nonstop. Connie thought she'd settle down when she married Roy's father and had the baby, but Theresa wasn't made for small-town life. When her husband was killed, she left Roy with her parents and she never came back."

"And Connie kept the locket all those years?" Frank asked.

"Yes, it was all she had of Theresa's father. She thought if she ever found Teresa again, she might tell her the truth. You know, to explain why she was so different from her sisters, and why she never really got along with Deke."

"But then Connie lost it."

Ardyth examined her African violets. "Yes, Connie didn't like to say, but I suspect Roy must have found it and took it to sell for drug money. He stole other things from them, you know."

"Uh-huh. So how did it wind up in the park?"

"I'm sure you're aware that people congregate there for illegal purposes," Ardyth said. "I found all sorts of terrible things on park cleanup day last year."

"Over behind the restrooms, not out in the open on the playground," Frank said.

Ardyth sat up straight with her hands folded tightly in her lap. "He's a drug addict, Frank. Who can predict what he's likely to do?"

Call Frank looked her in the eye. "Why was the clasp broken?"

"What?"

Frank pulled the locket out of his pocket. "See here? The loop that the hook fits into is completely ripped open. You know how I think that happened?"

Ardyth twisted her hands, her lips pressed shut.

"I think this locket was snatched off the neck of the woman wearing it. And Connie certainly never wore it anymore, did she?"

Ardyth flinched, as if he really had hit her. Frank pressed on.

"Roy took the locket, but he didn't steal it from his grandmother. He got into an argument in the park, an argument with his mother. He pulled this locket off Theresa's neck."

Ardyth's ramrod posture dissolved. "Out of the blue, Theresa contacted Connie last year. She was in AA and trying to make amends with people she'd hurt. Connie told her the truth about her father and sent her the locket, hoping it would help Theresa's recovery. But then Theresa wanted to come home and tell Deke and Roy the whole story. By that time, Roy was in the rehab place and Deke was footing the bill. Connie told her to wait —she was afraid of Deke's reaction, and she didn't want to jeopardize Roy's recovery. So Connie and Theresa argued again."

Frank rose and looked down at Ardyth. "When you told Connie about finding the locket, she realized it could only mean one thing. Theresa was back."

Ardyth stood and banged the cups and plates onto a tray. "Connie's had a hard life, Frank. If it turns out Theresa hurt Roy –" She pulled the mug from Frank's hand. "How much more suffering can a woman take? I had to help my friend. I would do it again."

"I can't believe this town." Frank plopped their donuts on his desk and poured two cups of Doris's sludge. "The temperature in the store dropped about twenty degrees when I walked in."

"Guess they all heard you arrested Theresa Corvin," Earl said, examining his choice of sweets.

"I'm sorry I couldn't oblige them by collaring some anonymous drug addict for shooting Roy. I must've missed the line in my contract that said, 'Only go after New York City scumbags passing through the Adirondacks on their way to Montreal.'"

"Everyone was hoping for a happy ending now that Roy's off the ventilator and out of ICU," Earl said. "It's hard to believe he was shot by his own mother."

"She's a volatile alcoholic. He's an angry drug addict. There's a gun in the mix. I'd say it was a toss-up who would be the victim and who the perp." Frank dunked his cruller in his coffee. "She might have gotten away with it if she hadn't used Mrs.

Nuegeberger's cell phone a second time. That made it easy to track her down in Syracuse."

"Couldn't resist calling the hospital to check on Roy. Ironic that Theresa would be tripped up by motherly love."

Frank crumpled the donut bag. "Honestly, I think she wanted to get caught. The cops who brought her in said she started confessing before they even had her in the patrol car." He believed that, so why didn't he feel the usual satisfaction in solving a difficult case?

"Maybe it's all for the best," Earl said. "Maybe the whole family can make a clean start now that the truth is out. Keeping secrets wears you down."

Frank tipped the dregs of his coffee into the terminally ill philodendron on the windowsill. "Earl, there's something I have to tell you."

"You wanted the jelly, not the cruller. Sorry."

"No, about the locket. I discovered it was missing right after Ardyth took it." Frank tossed the words out like he was bailing water from a boat. "I didn't say anything to you. Or Doris. When it reappeared in the drawer, minus the photo, I realized –"

"Oh."

The coffee pot sputtered. The fluorescent light hummed.

"I guess there are cases where the evidence is hard to accept," Earl said. "Because even people you know really well can surprise you."

Frank turned to face him. "I'm sorry."

Earl looked at him for a long moment. "Like I said, people can surprise you."

COYOTE JUSTICE

Marge Malone had her regulars well trained.

Locals were welcome to hang out in her diner--eating pie, drinking coffee, spreading gossip—but only during off-peak hours. Unfortunately, Saturday of Presidents Day weekend in the Adirondacks was on-peak from 6 AM to closing. Police Chief Frank Bennett had been crazy busy all day: two fender-benders, one spin-out, and a coatless, car-unloading couple locked out of the house they'd rented for the weekend. Now there was a lull in which he might soothe his growling stomach, but the diner was packed. He considered retreating when he heard a familiar laugh. The sound, bells descending a scale, inspired a wave of heat within him that had nothing to do with being overdressed in the steamy interior of the crowded restaurant.

He spotted Penny Stevenson dispensing paperback novels and jokes to a table of four seniors. The old folks gazed up at her as if Audrey Hepburn had been reincarnated before them.

As he hesitated in the doorway, more tourists pressed in behind him, forcing him directly into Penny's path.

She saw him, and a big smile crinkled her eyes and dimpled her cheeks. But she smiled like that for everyone, didn't she?

"How are the crowds at the library?" Frank asked.

"This is not a reading weekend. I'm thinking of closing early. I promised Edwin and Lucy I'd come over to the Inn and help them out."

"Not in the kitchen?" Penny freely admitted she was a lousy cook.

"Don't worry. Edwin won't let me come into actual contact with food. I'll just clear plates and load the dishwashers." She signaled to a mom and two kids across the room that she had something for them, then ducked her head to dig for it in her purse. "After we get everyone fed, we're going to hang out and have a few beers." Penny stopped rummaging and looked Frank straight in the eye. "You should join us."

A prickle of pleasure coursed through him but he quickly squelched it. Frank reminded himself, as he always did when he felt his heart quickening in her presence, that when he had been Penny's age—thirty-three—she had been a sixth grader selling Thin Mints to finance her trip to camp.

Penny prodded his arm. "C'mon Frank—say yes. You'll be ready for a beer by eleven."

"Unfortunately, eleven is right when my business is picking up."

Penny made a face. Was she really disappointed?

"Well, you have to eat, and you'll never get dinner from Marge. Come to the Inn and eat in the kitchen. I'll mess up the presentation on one of Edwin's plates and save it for you." Penny winked at him.

Before he could think of a reply, she had one toddler in her arms and another dragging her away by the leg. A cross-country skier slipped past him and nabbed the last seat at the counter.

Frank left hungry.

The town secretary's piercing voice stopped him at the door to his office. "Frank, there's a problem with those girls who run the organic farm—they hear music out in the woods," Doris said. "And some skier is stuck at Whiteface. Says, do we know where his wife is?"

Whiteface was in Wilmington, ten miles away. "Why's he calling us?"

"He claims he has a house here in Trout Run. Michael Moran. Never heard of him."

And if Doris hadn't heard of a person, he didn't exist.

"Give that call to Earl. And what do you mean, music in the woods?"

Doris made crazy circles at her temple. As far as she was concerned, organic farming put you in the same lunatic fringe as Scientologists and the Illuminati.

Handling both calls in the small office, Frank felt like he had earphones connected to two iPods playing a different tune in each ear. In his left ear one of the farmers—was it Jade or Anna, the loopy one or the sensible one?—was nattering about music, "It's probably nothing and I hate to bother you because I know you're busy, but it is strange....."

And in his right ear he could hear Earl's side of a conversation with the other caller. "No, there haven't been any serious accidents today, just a fender-bender in the Trail's End parking lot....No, not an SUV, two sedans...no, no ambulance calls either..."

"...We keep hearing music when we go outside to tend to the chickens."

"Loud music, like from a party?" Frank asked.

"No, not party music. And not that loud either..."

So why were they complaining?

"You're stuck at Whiteface because your wife never picked you up? Uh, no sir, there aren't any taxis up here in Trout Run and Wilmington..."

"It's that old song Frank Sinatra used to sing. 'New York, New York' but without the words, just the dum-dum. da-da-da-da. Over and over again..."

"and you called her and she doesn't answer?" Earl said. "We can check your house. Where do you live?"

"...and we only hear it, when the wind is blowing, and then it stops, and then it starts again. So we're worried that maybe..."

"High Ridge Road, up at the crest?" Earl verified. "That big green house? Yeah, I know it. Vacation home, right?"

"I'd go out and check myself, but we're making kohlrabi fritters and we have to keep an eye on them," Jade said.

Frank shouted across the office. "Earl, does he live next door to Jade and Anna's farm?"

"Yeah—how did you know?"

"Ask him what his wife's cellphone ringtone is."

"Huh?"

"Ask."

"He says, 'New York, New York'."

The little farmhouse clung to the rising slope of the ridge with a limited view of the valley. The two small fields in which the women grew vegetables in the short Adirondack summers occupied the flat land in front of the house. Behind the house were the chicken coop and a small barn for the goats. The woods began to the east of the outbuildings and continued behind the other houses on the higher part of the ridge. Frank parked the police department jeep at the end of the cleared drive and strapped on his snowshoes. Marching toward the woods he heard nothing but the rustling bows of the hemlocks and the soft murmuring clucks of the hens. The snow, which had been falling steadily since noon, had slowed to a few lazy flakes. In the distance, he heard the echo of a gunshot—someone hunting small game at dusk. Then through the cold, darkening air came the faint strains, "Dum, Dum, da-da-da-da, Dum-dum, da-da-da-da."

Around him, the snow-draped pines and birches stood impassive as Marines at attention. At intervals, the trees sported bright orange signs POSTED PRIVATE PROPERTY NO HUNTING" Frank forged a path through them, following the elusive strains of the music. He'd left Earl with two orders: tell Moran to keep calling his wife's cellphone, and contact the Department of Environmental Conservation. Even if Frank found the cell phone, they might need the DEC dogs to find Renee Moran. Because surely the woman and her phone were no longer together.

The music stopped, but Frank trudged on, not sure if he was getting closer to the lost woman or not. He saw no tracks in the snow, but if she had started out early in the day, her tracks might be filled. "Renee!" he shouted. "Renee, can you hear me?" Suddenly in the black and white landscape Frank's sweeping flashlight picked up a new color. Had he imagined the flash of blue? He ventured farther between the trees, acutely aware that he wasn't really dressed for deep snow bushwhacking.

He flashed his light into the trees. Two eyes glowed back at him. But they were not human. He pushed on as the fox scampered away.

A branch bowed with snow dumped its cold load on the back of Frank's neck. As he jerked in surprise, his flashlight illuminated the tip of a bright blue snowshoe binding.

The woman lay on her side with her arms flung outward, her feet pointed in two directions. A blanket of soft snow covered her.

Frank ran forward, then stopped. She hadn't taken a bad fall.

Carefully, he brushed the snow off her back. Between the shoulders of her sleek white jacket was a perfect black hole. Between her breasts, a crater.

Renee Moran's heart wept into the snow.

It would take half an hour for the state police to arrive to secure the scene. In his time alone with the body Frank tried not to think about the woman's family waiting at the ski slopes, but his imagination got the better of him. They'd probably started out impatient, then irritated, then worried, now panicked. He couldn't help remembering the afternoon his own wife had been felled by an aneurism, how annoyed he'd been when the furnace repairman had called him at work to say Estelle was not answering the door. How certain he'd been that his daydreaming wife had forgotten the appointment. How wrong.

When the EMTs arrived, Frank gladly left them to their work and took the shortest route out of the woods. He found himself in Vonn and Barb McGrath's back yard. Barb must've been watching from her window because she rushed out onto her deck, waving to him in the twilight. "What's going on, Frank? I called the farm and the girls said someone was lost in the woods. Is it a child?"

Frank held up a hand and trudged toward the golden lights of the house. At her back door, he pulled off his snowshoes and followed Barb into her kitchen.

"Put on a pot of coffee, Vonn. Frank's about frozen."

Vonn, a tall man in his seventies, shambled over to the counter and contemplated the coffee pot as if it were an electron microscope. A small TV flashed muted scenes of a snowbound Manhattan, and his gaze drifted to the screen. Barb, slightly younger and much livelier, nudged him out of the way. "I'll make the coffee, honey. You get out the mugs. And offer Frank some muffins."

Frank's antennae went up at the mention of food. He never had managed to get any lunch, and the McGrath's house was suffused with the lovely smell of recent baking. But he felt a jarring disconnect between the cozy kitchen with it's blue and yellow-checked curtains and gap-toothed grandkids' class pictures stuck to the fridge and the stark black, white, and red scene out back. Renee Moran had gone out for a hike and ended up dead. Her husband and kids were waiting for a woman who would never arrive. The high spirits of the snowy holiday weekend had melted in the heat of violence.

Nevertheless, when the promised muffin appeared, Frank ate. Between bites and swallows of strong, hot coffee, he drew information from the McGraths.

"How well do you know your neighbors?"

"Jade and Anna?" Barb bustled around the kitchen, wiping the already spotless counters. "Oh, they're lovely girls. Always giving me tomatoes and beans and squash in the summer. I try to pay them, but they won't take a cent."

"Hard workers," Vonn added.

"How about the family up the hill?"

"Oh, them. They're not from around here. Where did he say they're from, Vonn?"

"Jersey. They show up occasionally. Haven't talked to them since the summer."

"Sometimes they come by helicopter. Land right in the field beside the house." Barb shook her head and walked over to the kitchen's large bay window. "I see lights on up there now. They must be up for the weekend." She turned toward Frank. "Is it one of their kids lost out there? Oh, lord!"

As Frank's gaze followed Barb, he noticed something that had been covered by the open back door when he walked in.

A .30-30 Winchester rifle propped in the corner.

"You always keep your gun out like that?" he asked Vonn.

"I do until I kill that damn coyote that took our Spanky." Vonn scowled into his mug.

The coffee and muffin churned in Frank's stomach.

"Spanky was your dog?"

Barb's lip trembled. "The best little dog. A terrier mix—only twenty pounds. We let him out in the yard to pee before bedtime—" Barb began to sob.

Vonn continued the tale. "That damn coyote darted out from the woods and carried the little guy off right in front of our eyes. In October he took some chickens from the farm; in November he killed Mira and Tom Paulson's cat. When he took Spanky, that was the final straw. I called Rusty over at the DEC office. He said a coyote that preys on domestic animals is considered nuisance wildlife. I could shoot him anytime if I saw him on my land."

"And you saw him today?"

"Yeah, twice. Once he ran real quick, and then he come back—"

Barb gripped the edge of the counter. "Hush up, Vonn."

"Huh? Frank asked me about the coyote. I saw him—"

She whacked her husband sharply on the upper arm. "We got nothin' more to say. Vonn's just getting over a stroke. He can't be upset like this."

"Upset? I'm not upset. You're the one who was just crying over Spanky."

Barb jerked her head toward the dining room and Frank followed her while Vonn sat at the kitchen table and returned to watching the news.

"You tell me what happened out back." Barb's voice was fierce and low.

"Renee Moran was snowshoeing alone. We found her with a bullet through her chest."

Barb's lips shaped the word no.

For a solid week the shooting of Renee Moran was all anyone in Trout Run could talk about. On Sunday, everyone offered prayers for that poor woman. She was young, had kids who needed her. By Tuesday, underneath the stream of sympathy for the victim ran a stronger current of compassion for Vonn. First a hip replacement, then a stroke, now this. The accident just might be the end of him. Sometime Wednesday afternoon the blame game began. What was she doing back there all alone anyway? And who went into the woods in winter dressed all in white? She was from the city—she didn't know better. Well, stay in the city, then, if you're going to be that dumb.

If there were a few tree huggers who felt the coyote didn't deserve to be shot, they kept silent in public forums like Malone's and the Store. People quoted Section 11-0523 of the Environmental Conservation Law with great authority: coyotes that are injuring private property may be taken by the owner at any time in any manner. That city guy better not try to start trouble because he didn't have a leg to stand on.

Some said Jade and Anna should've taken care of the coyote when he first stole their chickens and spared unsteady old Vonn the task, but that met with eye rolls because those girls didn't even own a gun. Others said Renee had been trespassing but they got shouted down. Since when did anyone in the Adirondacks care if a neighbor crossed his land? Ah, but the Morans weren't real neighbors, were they? No one knew them; no one even knew when they were occupying their house. True neighbors would've been aware of the coyote, and would not have stumbled into the path of a bullet meant for that marauder. By Friday, public opinion and legal precedent were united: Vonn couldn't be faulted for the death of Renee Moran.

Saturday morning, people began talking about the weather again.

On a non-holiday weekend, Sunday nights were quiet in Trout Run. Frank sent Earl home in time for the weekly Davis family dinner, declining, as he always did, Earl's invitation to join them. The rowdy Sunday evening camaraderie of Earl's scrum of cousins and in-laws plunged Frank into a loneliness he kept at bay during the workweek. In the quiet of the deserted office, Frank revisited the moment in the diner last week when Penny had invited him to drink beer with her and Edwin and Lucy at the Inn. He felt a sharp twist of disappointment that the shooting behind the McGrath's house had kept him from going, followed by the quick burn of shame. He was alive. Penny was alive. There would be another day. Not so for Renee Moran.

His phone chirped the arrival of a text message. Speak of the devil—Edwin. *LEGO crisis. Olivia needs you. Dinner included.*

Be right there.

Frank whistled as he locked the office door. With any luck, Edwin wouldn't expect him to handle his daughter's LEGO crisis single-handedly.

"Frank's here!" Olivia shouted.

"I hear you have problems." Frank basked in the iron grip of her skinny arms. It was nice to be greeted so passionately. No sign of Penny. Only Edwin waving with his chin as he furiously whipped something in a bowl.

Olivia dragged him to a corner of the big kitchen where a small table held her latest creation. "This Hogwarts Castle model is messed up. The package doesn't have the right number of pieces."

Frank looked at the box. "5,500 pieces. Age 12 and up. Have you turned 12 since the last time I was here?"

Olivia poked him with her pink bunny-slippered foot. "You know I'm only nine. But I'm good enough to do the big ones, if I just had the right pieces." Her brow furrowed. "I need more of these kind of bricks to make the towers connect up. LEGO cheated me!"

"Hmmm. When all else fails, read the directions." Paging through the complex diagrams, Frank discovered where she had gone wrong. "Look honey, you used three-pronged gray bricks here when you should've used two-prong. That's why you're short of the bricks you need on this side."

Olivia's scowl deepened and she stamped her foot, making her bunny ears shake. "I should have been able to figure that out. I hate it when I do dumb things." She smacked the tower and sent bricks ricocheting through the kitchen.

"Hey! None of that," Edwin warned.

Frank pulled the little girl into a hug and murmured in her ear. "We all make mistakes, Olivia. And sometimes it can be hard to see them when we're too close. Or if we're sure that we're right."

She pulled back so she could study his face. "You ever make mistakes like that?"

Frank sighed. "All the time. You know what I try to do when something's not going the way it should?"

"What?"

"Take a little break, then come back and look at it with a fresh eye."

"Good idea," Edwin said. "Let's break for dinner and you can fix that tower afterwards."

Olivia cast a longing look at her castle. Frank could tell she wanted to jump right back into the fray. He took her hot little hand in his. "C'mon, let's eat."

Olivia bounded across the kitchen. "Guess what, Frank? You're not the only company we're having at dinner."

Frank worked to keep his voice bland. "Oh? Who else?"

"Two big kids and their dad. Do you think they're too old for LEGOs?"

Disappointment shot through him so viscerally he thought he might actually have gasped.

"Probably," Edwin answered Olivia. "You can ask them, but if they say no, don't beg.

Edwin dispatched Olivia to set the table. "I hope you don't mind. I invited Mike Moran and his kids for dinner. They could use a little company."

"You know them?"

"He used to stay at the Inn while the house up here was being remodeled. He'd pop up alone for the weekend to check on the work. Really nice. Super smart. Invented some kind of financial software program and now he's a gazillionaire. But a totally regular guy."

"I'm surprised they want to stay here after what happened. How come they're not back in New Jersey?"

S.W. Hubbard

"You didn't know? They sold the house in Summit to live up here full time. The shooting happened at the end of their first week in Trout Run. How horrible is that?"

"Mmm—awful." Frank wondered if he could possibly escape. This guest list was making a frozen dinner in front of his TV look mighty good.

Olivia popped back into the kitchen. "I need one more plate. I forgot that Penny's upstairs with Mom."

"Can I have a beer?" Frank stood in front of the open fridge for a moment to cool down. If this roller coaster continued, he'd be the next person primed for a stroke.

Frank had eaten at the Iron Eagle countless times, but he'd never been to a weirder dinner. First of all, the food was strange, even for Edwin. Once the guests were all settled around the crackling fire in the living room, Lucy passed the appetizers.

"What are these, Edwin?"

"Edamame, goat cheese, and baby beets."

Lucy looked apologetically at her teenage guests. "Would you guys like some chips and salsa?"

Sophie smiled, revealing flawless teeth, and crossed her coltish legs at the ankles. "No thank you. I like beets."

Frank hoped her brother would opt for the normal food and rescue them all, but Drew Moran gamely popped one of the red, green, and white concoctions in his mouth. The kid chewed and swallowed, then turned to ask Penny if she'd lived in Trout Run all her life.

As Frank recalled from the incident report filed on Renee Moran, Sophie was fourteen and Drew eighteen. Where were the black eye make-up and the slutty clothes? Where were the sullen slumps, and the muttering, and the refusal to meet an adult's eye? Weird.

The conversation lurched along in strained politeness. What can you say to a man whose wife died in a freak accident? What chit-chat can you make with kids who just lost their mom? Every possible avenue of discourse—skiing, home remodeling, Adirondack pastimes—seemed inevitably to lead back to the woman missing from the group.

Finally, Olivia couldn't take it any more. "Sophie, do you like Harry Potter?"

"I love him."

Olivia grabbed the older girl's hand. "Good. Then you'll want to see the Hogwarts castle I'm building from LEGO."

Sophie rose. "Drew's the one who's really good with LEGO."

"He can come too." Olivia led the older kids off.

As soon as they were out of sight, Drew Moran threw his head back on the sofa. A tall, wiry man in his early forties, Moran looked more like a high school track coach than a software titan. "I can't bear this. The kids are being so good. They're holding themselves together for me. We should never have come."

Moran's outburst cut the tension. At least they no longer had to avoid the forbidden topic.

"Don't feel that way, " Lucy said. "You're among friends here. Just go ahead and vent."

Moran offered a weak smile. "Thank you. I meant we should never have moved to Trout Run."

The rest of them exchanged glances. Penny forged ahead. "Why *did* you decide to move up here full time? It's a big switch from Summit, New Jersey."

Mike Moran's gaze traveled around the room. Frank couldn't tell if Moran felt cornered by their interest, or baffled, as if he didn't know himself why he'd come.

Penny smiled and leaned forward, elbows on knees, head in hand. "All of us are transplants. We all came the Adirondacks looking for something. Some days, we even feel like we might have found it."

For a moment, Penny looked wistful. The interest and intensity she'd focused on Moran wavered and she slipped inside herself. Then her customary cheer returned.

"We're the NFAH support group, right Frank?"

"Not From Around Here," Frank explained. "It takes a few generations to become native North Country."

Moran eased back into his chair. "We came here for our kids. Funny how when you have kids, you want to make sure you don't make any of the mistakes your own parents made. So you lean so far in the other direction that you wind up in a place you don't even recognize. That's what Summit had become to us."

"Did you grow up there?" Edwin asked.

"No, Summit is a place where everyone is NFAH. You move there to erase the tiny little split level of your childhood."

Moran found his voice. His casual lankiness morphed into a wiry intensity. Frank could sense the fierce intellect that had launched a company and earned him millions.

"My dad was a teacher and my mom a social worker. They were very serious people, not at all frivolous. We weren't poor, but they were very thrifty. As kids, my sisters and I never had the trendy stuff the other kids had. And if we did succeed in wheedling a pair of Nikes or some new CDs out of our parents, they'd manage to make us feel like we were taking the food from the mouths of starving orphans. My older sister even had to get her prom dress at the resale shop. I still remember her crying that there was no way to get the Goodwill smell out of it."

"They wanted you to not be materialistic, but they went overboard," Lucy said.

"Exactly, but you can understand that when Renee and I had kids, I wanted them to have nothing but the best—the biggest house, the most prestigious school, the nicest clothes, every toy, every opportunity—they wouldn't want for a thing."

He looked at the group. "Have you ever been to Summit?"

Lucy nodded. "When Edwin and I lived in the city, I worked with a woman who lived there. Fabulous homes."

"All that loveliness comes with a cost: the competition, the status, the one-upmanship. Exhausting. A few years of that, and my parents' values didn't seem so bad after all. We needed a break, so we bought our place up here. We loved it, so we started spending more time in Trout Run. Finally we decided to make the move, and then...." He swallowed hard and gazed into the fire. "It's my fault. It's all my fault."

When Michael Moran choked up, Lucy and Penny began fluttering, two beautiful butterflies circling a drooping flower. While the women fussed, Frank observed their target. The get-away-from- the–rat- race scenario seemed off. Would teenagers sophisticated enough to eat goat cheese and edamame embrace the 4H Club culture at High Peaks High School? It was hard to transplant kids at that age. Their roots were too tenacious to easily release the soil in which they had first sprouted, and too fragile to readily take hold in new dirt.

And why was Moran blaming himself for his wife's death? Surely a liberal suburbanite would be tempted to pin this tragedy on rural gun culture.

Frank tried to catch Edwin's eye for some sign that he agreed Moran's performance was over-the-top. But Edwin looked just as concerned as the ladies, and Frank had to ask himself why he was so suspicious. Occupational hazard? Or maybe watching Penny murmuring reassurances to a handsome, wealthy, smart younger man brought out the worst in him.

Once the party moved to the dining room, the mood lightened and the food improved. Edwin served butternut squash soup, which, despite a suspicious orange hue, was quite tasty. Olivia regaled them with tales of her plans to design and build her own medieval castle.

"I'm going to work it out myself and order the exact bricks I need direct from LEGO. Then I don't have to follow their dumb old rules."

Mike Moran high-fived Olivia. "Awesome! Do you know that's what Drew is going to do for next few months? He's designed his own engineering project and he's going to work on that instead of going to school. He's already been admitted early decision to MIT."

Frank observed the faces at the table. Moran beamed with paternal pride. Lucy and Edwin were clearly impressed. Penny leaned forward, eyes gleaming. "How exciting! Tell me all about your project."

Drew studied his plate, nudging the salmon away from the peas. "It's a software thing. Some guy from my dad's office is going to help me."

"My lead software engineer has agreed to mentor Drew," Moran jumped in to explain.

Frank watched the father-son dynamic. Drew's social skills had dissipated like dew on a sunny lawn once his father started boasting about this special project. The kid who'd been chatting quite easily with the adults now fell mute.

"No senior slump for you," Penny said. "Will you go back to your school for prom and graduation parties?"

Both Drew and his sister had an arresting combination of fair skin and dark hair, so when two rosy patches appeared on the boy's cheeks, Frank noticed.

"Nah," Drew buttered a dinner roll with neat, even strokes. "That's kinda what we're trying to get away from. People at my school go off the deep end with parties—renting limos, chartering sailboats. I'm just going to chill up here. Ski...hike...maybe learn to fish."

Frank focused on plucking the peas from his otherwise delicious risotto. Since when did a handsome teenage boy choose a canoe and a bucket of worms over a sailboat full of drunken girls?

"What about you, Sophie? Where will you be going to school?" Lucy asked.

"I'm home-schooling her," her father answered. "Maybe next fall she'll go to boarding school."

Sophie sat with a ballerina's ramrod posture, her smile so slight it hardly required the use of muscles. "I noticed you do craft hour at the library, Penny. Maybe I could help you with that. I like art."

"Fabulous! I'm always looking for helpers. Last fall Frank made me twenty of the sweetest little wooden bird houses for the kids to paint, but I can't hit him up for another favor until June at the earliest." Penny tilted her head and pulled a mock woeful face.

"Penny, I'm pretty sure you can get Frank to do anything, anytime," Edwin said.

Under the tablecloth, Penny rested her hand on Frank's knee. He felt his blood coursing through his veins. Her head tilted toward his and he could smell the fresh flowers of her shampoo.

Penny whispered in his ear. "Eat your peas."

Mike Moran's unwavering gaze bored into Frank.

"I don't have much time." Marcy Ann McGrath Rayborn plopped into a chair across from Frank. Her flushed face peeked out from an oversize man's parka. Curly, reddish hair stood up in static-y tufts when she pulled off her hat. "I'm in town to pick my son up from work. After I drop him off, I head to my job. We only have the one car."

After the recent collapse of her marriage, Marcy Ann and her teen-aged son had moved in with Barb and Vonn. Frank knew Marcy Ann's husband, Tom Rayborn, because he'd been at the wrong end of a few fights at the Mountainside Tavern. No doubt, Marcy Ann was better off without him.

She leaned across the desk. Frank guessed she was barely forty, but worry and disappointment had etched her face. "I'm concerned about my dad, Frank. He doesn't want to get out of bed in the morning. He gets more depressed every day."

Frank nodded and hoped he had dialed up the correct expression of empathy. When he had taken the police chief's job, no one had warned him that he'd become a part-time family therapist in the bargain.

"He told mom he feels like life ain't worth living. We're afraid to let him out of our sight. I locked up all the guns and I got the key in the vault." She patted her substantial bosom.

"Mrs. Moran's death is a tragic accident, Marcy Ann. Don't worry—your dad's not going to be charged. But it's natural for Vonn to feel bad even though he didn't do anything wrong."

"He didn't shoot her Frank! I keep telling the state police and the DEC and no one will listen."

Marcy Ann's voice had the ragged pitch of a foreign tourist who despairs of ever making the taxi driver understand where she wants to go. To stave off hysteria, Frank patted her hand. "I'm listening. You go ahead and tell me."

"Here's the thing: I know exactly what time he fired the gun in the morning. It was 8:15 during the Today show...the Martha Stewart segment on how to get a bundt cake to pop out of the pan. I stopped what I was doing to watch because I always have trouble with those damn cakes sticking. And then I glanced out the window and saw the coyote and told Dad. And he went out and took his shot. He thought he mighta winged the coyote, but he wasn't sure. And by the time all that happened, Martha was off and I never did hear her tip on the bundt cake. And that's how I know that Dad fired the shot while that woman was still dropping her family off at Whiteface." Marcy Ann sat back in her chair with an unspoken "ta-da".

Frank knew she expected a big reaction but all he could muster was a slight raise of his eyebrows. "Did you hear another shot behind your house later in the morning?"

Marcy Ann bit her lip. "Mom and I went out grocery shopping. Dad was home all alone. He can't remember what he heard. And neither can Jade and Anna."

Frank nodded. The echo of a hunting rifle was so common that it simply didn't register in people's conscious minds. "What did Lt. Meyerson say?" He asked knowing full well that the state trooper in charge had dismissed Marcy Ann's claim as wishful thinking after the fact.

"Meyerson's the one with the squinty eyes, right? He wouldn't let me be in the room when he talked to Dad. Then he came out and said Dad wasn't certain what time he fired the shot. That's the problem, Frank. Since his stroke, my father has a hard time remembering things. He gets mixed up real easy. I listened through the den door, and that guy just kept hammering Dad with questions until the poor man didn't know if he was coming or going. Then when I told Meyerson the god's honest truth, he didn't want to believe me!"

Frank sat quietly. They could argue all day about what time Vonn took his pot shot at the coyote. Nothing changed the fact that Renee Moran died from a gunshot wound consistent with a .30-30 rifle 100 yards into the woods behind Vonn's house. The bullet, which would have been conclusive proof, had passed right through her. Buried in six feet of snow, it might never be found.

"Well? Why are you just sitting there?"

Frank raised his hands palms up. "Your land is posted No Hunting. No one poaches small game. If Vonn didn't kill her, who did?"

"That's what I want you to find out. Why are you swallowing whatever the state police say?" Marcy Ann glanced at her watch and jumped up as a young man appeared in the office doorway.

"Jeff! I didn't mean to make you wait. We can go right now."

"Hey, Jeff—How's it goin'?" Earl said.

The kid glanced at Earl and barely nodded. He was tall and rangy, with the startled look of a young man confounded by the size of his own arms and legs. To top it off, he had the worst case of acne Frank had ever seen. Frank's cheeks felt sore just looking at him.

Marcy Ann yanked her hat down over her ears. "What's the point of Trout Run having its own police department if you're not looking out for us?" She shepherded her son through the door, then glanced back at Frank. "I can't watch over my dad twenty-four hours a day, Frank. If something happens to him, it'll be on you."

Earl let out a long whistle once the outer door had slammed. "If a crazy old man who can't remember what time he shot his gun decides to kill himself, it's your fault, Frank. Geez—glad I'm not Chief."

Frank stared at the bulletin board of out-of-date wanted posters.

"What?" Earl asked when he couldn't take the silence any longer.

"Vonn gets more and more upset about the accident with every passing day. Meanwhile, everyone expects Moran to be looking for someone to sue. But he's remarkably forgiving. In fact, he blames himself. Why?"

"I dunno. Guess he's nicer than most rich people."

"Rich or poor, hurt people like to assign blame. But he's not."

"So...?"

"What if Marcy Ann's right? She's seems totally sure what time Vonn fired the shot."

"My mom watches Martha Stewart on the Today show. That segment comes on a couple of different times during the morning. I think Marcy Ann just confused Vonn's shot with the earliest Martha segment because that's when she wanted it to be. The bottom line is, if not Vonn, who? Those organic farming girls don't even own a gun. The Paulsons were in Florida. You always tell me that if I hear hoofbeats, think horses, not zebras."

Frank raised his eyebrows. "A husband killing his wife isn't a zebra."

"Moran was skiing at Whiteface all day."

"Was he? Meyerson says the dad and kids were skiing together all day, but is there any evidence that proves the three of them were never out of each other's sight? It's pretty hard to always stay together when you're skiing. And what teenagers want to ski with their slow old man?"

Earl leaned forward. "How would he have gotten to the woods and then back to the slopes? Renee had the SUV."

"Moran is rich and smart. We're not used to dealing with that combo."

Earl crossed the office and rattled the locked bottom drawer of the file cabinet. "Is the weed we confiscated from that party last week still in here? I think you've been smokin' something, man."

Frank entered the library at ten minutes before closing time. No more agonizing; today he would ask Penny out. The way she'd put her hand on his knee during dinner at the Inn—he couldn't be mistaken—she was interested. He assumed she'd be alone this late in the day, but as he walked past the stacks he could hear Penny's animated voice.

"The best part of any journey by plane, boat or train is when it is over and you are…"

"Home again!" two shrill voices piped. "Read it again, Penny!"

Frank stood just outside the doorway to the activity room and peeped in. Penny sat in the oversized easy chair with a skinny child tucked on either side of her. One kid pushed her tangled brown hair back so she could see *Madeline and the Gypsies* more clearly. The other flipped the pages back to the beginning and prodded Penny to start.

"All right, girls. One more time, then home you go."

As Frank watched the little tableau, molten lead rose up to the back of his throat, pulling down his shoulders, spreading an ache through his back. He would be fifty next month. He'd never cared much about his birthdays, but suddenly he felt the terrible rush of time. More than half his life was over. He had grandchildren. He was old.

Who was he kidding? He was not the right man for Penny. Even if she sometimes flirted with him, he would be wrong to encourage her. Seeing these two little urchins curled up with Penny, Frank was struck by how glad he was not to be their father. He adored his grandsons, but he was always a little relieved to regain his solitude after a visit. Kids required constant attention, produced endless worry, sucked up boundless energy. He was done with that phase of his life; he couldn't—didn't want to—start it again. But Penny deserved to have children; she'd make a wonderful mother.

He stood rooted to the spot listening to her voice rise and fall, doing what his wife used to call "pre-worrying." He and Penny had never even been on an official date, and here he was concerned about marriage and babies. But if things between them didn't work out—and how could they, really?—he and Penny would still have to see each other day in and day out. Yet walking away seemed equally impossible. This constant tension, this waiting for the other shoe to drop, was killing him.

He backed away from the activity room, still not certain if he should wait for Penny or just slip out the door. Standing now before Penny's desk, his gaze fell on a bright red rectangle: DATAVERGENT SOLUTIONS, MICHAEL MORAN, FOUNDER & CEO. Frank turned the business card over. On the back Moran had scrawled, "Call me," and another phone number, presumably a private line. Frank quickly copied both numbers onto the back of a bookmark, and as Penny and the girls were shouting "Home again!" for the second time, Frank slipped out the library door.

Frank and Rusty stared down at the slushy snow. Between them lay a body, frozen stiff.

"How long do you think it's been here?" Frank asked the DEC officer.

"Hard to say. We had almost eight inches of snow early last week. Then the thaw started two days ago. The coyote's been buried in snow and well preserved. " Rusty used a stick to point at the matted beige fur. "You can see he was hit in the thigh. The shot didn't kill him right away. He ran for a bit, then crawled behind this log for protection. He eventually bled out, and the snow covered him and the trail of blood he must have left."

"You're sure this is the coyote Vonn shot at?"

"You can't put a wild animal in a line-up, Frank, but the farmers and Vonn described a large male coyote. This one's about as big as I've seen in the Adirondacks. A dominant male doesn't let other adult males on his territory. "

"I thought coyotes ran in packs."

"No, they're not like wolves. They live in a family unit: mother, father, and pups. Now is the time of year that the adult male runs off the male pups, forces them to find their own territory. But this guy is a mature adult. I'd say he weighs forty-five, fifty pounds."

Frank crouched down to look closely at the animal without touching it. "I don't see an exit wound. If the bullet is still in there, we'll be able to know for sure if Vonn's shot killed it." Frank rocked back on his heels and stared up at Rusty. "What's the likelihood that Vonn's one bullet would pass through Renee Moran and then lodge in this coyote?"

Rusty's long exhale produced a cloud in front of his freckled face. "I suppose it depends on whether we're going to start believing Vonn's version of events. If he really saw the coyote at the verge of the woods, took his shot, and hit the animal, then Mrs. Moran would have to have been standing out in the open, between Vonn and the coyote, for the bullet to pass through her and hit its intended mark. But if Vonn just fired blindly into the woods after the coyote took off, then I suppose it could've gone through her before it hit this guy."

Frank gazed through the bare branches toward Vonn's house. "What are the chances that one wild potshot hit two targets?"

Frank waited until Earl had left for the morning patrol before picking up his cell phone. The discovery of the dead coyote had changed the case. His suspicions weren't crazy. The bullet from the coyote would be tested to determine if it came from Vonn's gun. But that test, which would take at least a week, wouldn't shed light on what gun had killed Renee. Frank still needed to determine if Drew Moran had any reason to kill his wife before he could recruit the state police to help find the circumstantial evidence. His hand hovered over the phone. Why was he doing this? To help Vonn, of course. The poor old man shouldn't have to live with the guilt of having killed someone if he hadn't really done it.

Liar.

He could accept the idea of Penny being with another man, a younger man who could give her kids, but he was damned if that man would be a killer. Penny had suffered enough in her first marriage. She deserved a good, honest guy. If there was even a shadow of doubt in Frank's mind that Mike Moran had something to do with his wife's death, he'd protect Penny from that man. He might never find enough evidence to convict the guy, but if he uncovered anything suspicious, he'd use it to drive Moran off.

Last night, Frank had searched the Internet for information on the exclusive private school the Moran kids attended— Moorewood Academy. The school's website showed the usual array of wholesome kids, but these kids studied Mandarin Chinese, molecular chemistry, and Greek philosophy to the tune of fifty grand a year. Maybe Drew's independent study project made sense, but why would the Morans have pulled Sophie out of such a place to teach her at their kitchen table? Something had caused the family to leave New Jersey and Frank was determined to find out what. But headmasters don't spill their guts about students who pay top dollar. Frank pulled out a scrap of paper with a name and number he'd found on the website: Moorewood Parent Partnership League, Genevieve Llewellyn, Chair.

Frank dialed. "This should be fun."

Chatting up his new best friend, he managed to imply that he was very close to the family whose name graced the Moorewood Library. That of course he knew the school's academic reputation was sterling, but that when it came to sending his beloved Beatrice there, he had to be certain the atmosphere was conducive to her happiness. He had heard rumors of some recent unpleasantness. Could Genevieve set his mind at ease?

Genevieve was a cagey one, and they had to waltz around the dance floor several times, but every turn brought her a little closer to spilling all she knew. Yes, she finally admitted, there had been a problem. An incident of physical aggression. Of course violence was never the answer, but under the circumstances.....

"Bullying?" Frank inquired.

Genevieve was shocked. "No, No! Nothing of that sort. All the parties involved are gone now. There's no need for concern."

"But I just can't rest easy until I understand the reason for the aggression." Frank warmed to his role. A pity Earl couldn't hear the performance. "Beatrice is such a sensitive child. She couldn't be happy in a community that condones violence."

"I assure you Mr. Bennett, Moorewood has a zero tolerance policy against physical encounters. That's why the young man in question was asked to leave. It's just, well, it's a shame because he reacted—inappropriately for sure—but understandably, to a situation that was beyond his control."

"What situation?"

But Genevieve Llewellyn wouldn't be moved an inch further. "The family in question has recently experienced a tragedy. No good can come of discussing this further. They've suffered enough."

"Guess who I gave a speeding ticket to?" Earl asked, breezing back into the office.

"Please don't tell me you collared that poor little Polish priest from St. Andrew's in Verona. The Knights of Columbus will have my ass."

"Nah. I scared him so bad last time, now he causes a traffic jam wherever he goes. It was Jeff Rayborn going eighty on Route 9."

"Eighty! I can't believe that beater minivan of his mother's could get above sixty."

"That's the crazy thing. He was driving a brand new red Mazda MR6. Still has dealer plates. I thought it was some tourist when I pulled him over. Coulda knocked me over when I saw it was Jeff."

Earl had Frank's full attention now. "Who was the car registered to?"

"Jeff Rayborn. He told me his dad bought it for him."

"His dad? His dad can't afford to pay his bar tab at the Mountainside."

Earl looked fit to explode. He pulled a folded copy of the *Mountain Herald* from his back packet and unfurled the weekly newspaper with a flourish. "Trout Run Man Wins State Lottery," the headline read.

Frank scanned the article. Apparently Tom Rayborn had won a hundred thousand dollars on a ticket purchased at a convenience store on the Northway just outside Albany.

Frank sat holding the paper, his eyes no longer focused on the type.

"What's the matter?" Earl asked. "Don't you think it's nice something good finally happened to someone in the McGrath family? "

"Yeah. Looks like their luck has turned." Frank stuck the newspaper under his desk blotter. "I wouldn't peg Tom as a guy who'd buy his son a foreign sports car. Or Jeff to want one, for that matter. Wouldn't a new pick-up be more useful?"

"For hunting, yes." Earl leered as he headed back out. "But maybe Jeff has his sights set on something nicer than a six point buck."

Once Earl was gone, Frank pulled out the paper again. The rag's motto was "The North Country's Good News Paper," but Frank thought it should be "Yesterday's news, next week." There were still old ladies who liked to clip out wedding announcements and stories about their grandkids starring in the class play, but once those old gals passed on, the *Mountain Herald* would probably die too, no doubt replaced by a High Peaks Twitter account. By the time news appeared in the *Herald*, it had already been thoroughly discussed at Malone's, the Store, and the Presbyterian Church fellowship hour. How could it be that Tom had won the Lottery and Earl hadn't known anything about it until he'd read it in the paper?

He called the *Herald* and got Greg Faraday, editor, reporter, photographer, designer, ad salesman, and receptionist.

"Quite a story about Tom winning the Lottery. How'd you get the news?"

"From Tom, how else? You can see I took his picture with the winning ticket."

"It's just a Lotto ticket. How do you know it's really a winner?"

Greg spoke with exaggerated patience. "Tom told me the name of the place where be bought it and I called to verify. Kwik-Valu, right off Exit 24."

"And they said they sold Tom a ticket worth a hundred grand?"

"They don't know who they sold it to. They just said they sold a big winner last week."

"They confirmed the sale of a hundred thousand dollar ticket?" Frank pressed.

"The guy was foreign—Indian or Chinese or something. He just kept saying, 'Yes, yes, big winnah.' You don't believe Tom really won? Call the Lotto Commission if you want proof. I got another line ringing here." And he was gone.

Frank took Greg's advice. But tracking down the right Lottery bureaucrat to squeeze for information was no easy matter. No, he didn't have a warrant. Please hold. No, he wasn't a state officer. Please hold. As he listened to the canned hold music for the third time, Frank gazed out the window. The Nativity statues had finally been taken down for the season, so the Green looked forlornly empty and would stay that way until the garden committee began their ministrations in May. The recent warm snap had melted a lot of snow, and gray slush formed a dismal ribbon around the park. The only bright spot was the cheery red door of the town library. As he watched, the door opened and Penny stepped out, accompanied by another woman even more slender than she. Together, they wrestled a large sign out the door and set it up at the end of the sidewalk. Frank knew what it said: AFTER SCHOOL STORY HOUR WITH MISS PENNY. Before Christmas, at Penny's behest, he'd used his jigsaw to cut a large piece of plywood into the shape of an open book. Penny had painted it and launched her initiative to get the kids of Trout Run out from in front of their TVs. The usual naysayers had insisted the program wouldn't work, but now, two months in, Penny had more kids at the library than she could ride herd on. Apparently she'd found a helper.

With the Lottery Commission hold music still playing in his ear, Frank squinted and realized the other person was Sophie

Moran. Of course—at dinner she'd asked about volunteering. Now Frank could see Penny gesturing. An SUV with New Jersey plates pulled up to the curb. Mike Moran hugged his daughter. Then he raised his left hand toward the small of Penny's back. Frank tensed. Moran's hand dropped without making contact. All three turned and went into the library.

The hold music stopped. The line clicked.

Dial tone.

Frank fought an uphill battle to like his son-in-law. One of the qualities that annoyed him most in Caroline's husband was Eric's boundless circle of connections. If you told him you needed a two-headed unicorn with a purple tail, in a few clicks of his iPhone he'd track down someone who knew someone who knew someone else who could get it for you wholesale. Nevertheless, that network might come in handy right now. Surely Eric—Mr. Wall Street—would know someone with the inside scoop on Michael Moran and his high-tech start-up.

That night, after fifteen minutes of small talk with Caroline and the requisite unintelligible chat with his toddler grandsons, Frank finally got to ask Eric what he knew about Mike Moran.

"Word on the street is he wants to step down as CEO of DataVergent and get into politics. You know—become the next Mike Bloomberg."

"So why move up here?"

"Probably figures it's cheaper to buy a seat in Congress in an upstate New York district than in New Jersey. The northern New Jersey media market is astronomical."

Frank was glad Eric couldn't see him making faces on the other end of the phone. After all, he'd called his son-in-law precisely to get this kind of information, but he couldn't help being irritated that Eric actually knew all this stuff.

"So if he's planning a run for office, he'd naturally want to avoid any hints of scandal," Frank continued. "But it seems his son was kicked out of this fancy prep school—Moorewood Academy. You heard of it?"

Eric made the sound that never failed to raise Frank's hackles—a cross between a snort and a laugh that managed to convey contempt and pity and superiority without resorting to words whatsoever. "Of course. It's one of the most prestigious prep schools in the country. Right up there with Choate and Sidwell Friends." He paused. "You know, where the president's kids go."

Frank took a calming breath.

"But the kid's flunking out of Moorewood wouldn't be enough to damage his father's political prospects," Eric said.

"He didn't flunk out. According to the PTA lady, there was some sort of 'aggressive incident', but she wouldn't share the details."

Again with the snort. "I got this. A guy I work with is an alum. Call you back in a few."

Frank got up from his easy chair and allowed himself a rare treat—half a glass of Jim Beam, neat. One good thing about Eric— he was so disinterested in his father-in-law's boring, small-town job, he never even asked why Frank wanted to know so much about Mike Moran. By the time the warm glow of the bourbon unkinked the knot in his neck, his phone was ringing.

"Listen to this. Drew Moran attacked the lacrosse coach who was having an affair with his mother."

Frank's heart rate kicked up. This was it. He tempered the excitement in his voice. "Ahh—poor kid. His coach was nailing his mother. A double betrayal."

"Not *his* coach. His *sister's* coach. Loretta Kolb."

Frank nursed his bourbon by the dying the fire in his living room, twisting his glass this way and that, studying the refractions of firelight. Surely what Eric had told him gave Mike Moran a motive for murder. It would have been bad enough for Moran to have discovered his wife's infidelity. But to know your wife was cheating on you with another woman—a man would have a hard time recovering from that. Yet the Morans had decided to stay together. Still, could Mike ever feel truly confident that he'd won his wife back?

And then there was the complication of Mike Moran's political ambitions. With a lesbian affair not very neatly tucked in the closet, the possibility for scandal would always be there. How could he launch his political career with that hanging over his head?

Frank swirled the remaining bourbon in his glass. Maybe it wasn't such a big a deal. After all, voters had forgiven far worse: Bill Clinton, Elliott Spitzer, Mark Sanford. But even if Renee's affair didn't keep Mike from getting elected, it would certainly be dredged up during the campaign. He wasn't just anyone running for Congress. He was Mike Moran—handsome, brilliant, software wunderkind multi-millionaire. The whole family would have to cope with a media machine that loved finding dirt on people who seem too good to be true.

Frank knocked back the last of the Jim Beam. Mike Moran was an entrepreneur, a problem-solver. Maybe he saw death-by-tragic-accident as a way to wipe the family slate clean.

Friday morning Frank woke eager to share his new information with the state police. But the day started off with not one but two knocked-down road signs, continued with a shoplifting incident, escalated to a domestic disturbance, and wound down with the usual end of the work-week rowdiness at the Mountainside Tavern.

Frank swung by at ten to find trouble already in progress, courtesy of Tom Rayborn.

"Get him outta here," the bartender said. "He's messed up on something real bad."

"What?"

The bartender shrugged. "He was high as a kite when he came in. I wouldn't serve him, but then it got crowded and some guy from Verona started buying rounds. Turned out he was using Tom's money to buy shots and beer for Tom and ten other people. I want him outta here before he starts something."

George Strait blared from the jukebox and a few people danced near the pool tables. Tom lurched spastically across the dance floor, crashing into tables, knocking over chairs. One man shoved Tom away from a woman, causing him to careen toward another couple. Frank stepped in just as the man was about to take a swing.

"Hold up, buddy. Let me get him out of your way." The crowd parted, and Frank grabbed Tom by the belt and collar and prepared to haul him out to the squad car.

"You finally got a partner to two-step with you," a wise-guy at the bar shouted.

Tom struggled to free himself. "You a-holes don't want me dancin' with your women 'cause I'm too hot."

The crowd roared, enjoying the show.

"But my money's good enough to buy you drinks. You mothers gonna miss me when I'm gone."

Frank dragged him a few steps closer to the door. "You planning a trip?"

Tom's knees wobbled and he steadied himself against the side of a booth. "I'm thinkin' I'll fly somewhere warm. Sick of this damn snow."

"You still have money enough for that?"

"Sure, man—I gotta hundred grand."

"Seventy grand after taxes," Frank said. "Sixty for that fancy car for Jeff. And all these rounds at the Mountainside. Seems to me you might have to take the Greyhound to Florida."

Tom's laughter ended in a defiant shout. "I ain't payin' no taxes, man. An' there's plenny more money where this come from."

Someone opened the bar door and Frank and Tom stumbled out into the cold night.

Tom was quiet during the ride back to the office, but Frank had a hell of a time hauling the semi-conscious man into the holding cell. He briefly considered calling the EMTs, but he doubted they'd be willing to drive Tom to the hospital in Saranac Lake to have his stomach pumped since the drunk's pulse was strong and steady. Frank dumped his charge on the bunk and straightened his legs out. In the process, Tom's cell phone slid from his pocket and clattered to the floor.

Frank cradled it in his hand.

What had Tom meant when he said he didn't have to pay taxes on his winnings? What had he meant when he said there was plenty more money to come? Frank wished he'd been more persistent with the Lottery Commission. Had Tom Rayborn really claimed a hundred thousand dollar winning ticket? If Tom's new wealth hadn't come from the Lottery, there was only one other plausible source. Frank checked the phone's contacts list—no Mike Moran listed. He pulled out the bookmark where he'd written Mike Moran's two phone numbers and compared them to the numbers in Tom's recent calls list. There were no matches. But one number showed up repeatedly on Tom's recently called list. It had the same 908 New Jersey area code as Mike Moran's numbers. It even had the same exchange as Mike's private line. Only the last digit was different.

Another private line. One that Mike Moran used to contact Tom Rayborn.

Frank tried to shake Tom back to consciousness with no success. Finally he held a cold soda can to Tom's temple and the man's eyelids fluttered.

"Where did you get the money, Tom? I know there was no winning lottery ticket."

Tom's pupils were as huge and black as a night-prowling cat's. He twisted his head, searching for the source of the question. "I hadda ticket. He givva to me."

"Who?"

Tom's jaw gaped and he collapsed in a heap. This time there was no reviving him.

Frank studied the pathetic drunk sprawled on the cot. Moran had hired this man to kill the mother of his children. Not a crime of passion, one of cold-blooded calculation. Moran was accustomed to success. His wife had made a dangerous mistake when she humiliated him.

Clearly a few hours needed to pass before anyone could interrogate Tom Rayborn. Frank turned the man on his side so he wouldn't choke if he vomited. But before he summoned the state police, there was someone he needed to talk to.

Frank cruised down the tiny side street where Penny lived. Lights glowed in the first floor windows. In their golden radiance he could make out a car parked in the driveway. A large black SUV with New Jersey plates.

He pounded on Penny's front door. The steps that had brought him from his car to this spot melted into a white blur of anger.

Inside, he could hear movement. The porch light came on and the living room curtain twitched. A moment later, Penny flung open the door.

"Frank! What are you doing here? Is something wrong?"

He pushed past her into the hallway, searching for Moran.

Penny tailed him into the living-room. "Frank?"

Moran rose awkwardly from the low, soft sofa. His hair looked disheveled. Two glasses with puddles of red wine in the bottoms stood on the coffee table, next to a plate with a half-eaten wedge of cheese.

Frank knew his emotions were war paint smeared across his face.

Penny stood with her hands on her hips, somewhere between irritated and amused.

"Rough night, Frank?"

"As a matter of fact, I have had a rough night. I had to haul Tom Rayborn out of the Mountainside. Drunk as a skunk, talking crazy, and making a scene. He's been nothing but trouble since he won the Lottery."

Frank watched Moran for a reaction, and was rewarded with a look of bland boredom. He kept talking. "Old Tom seems to be running through his prize money pretty quickly, but tonight he kept insisting there was plenty more where that came from. But I don't think he meant he was going to win the Lottery again."

Still no reaction.

Penny's expression darkened. "Why are you telling us this, Frank?"

He turned to face her. "Do you know why Drew and Sophie dropped out of their fancy private school?"

That got a reaction from Moran. "Look Bennett, what right do you have to snoop in my—"

Frank kept his eyes glued on Penny. "Do you?"

She took a step back from the two angry men. "Drew was bored. Sophie was having some trouble with mean girls."

"Do you know why they were mean?"

"I went to boarding school--teenage girls don't need a reason. They're hungry sharks."

"These particular sharks were feeding on some juicy gossip. Do you want to know what it is?"

"No! No, I don't. What's gotten into you, Frank? You're being outrageously cruel. You need to leave."

"Listen to me, Penny. I'm only trying to protect you. His wife was having an affair...an affair with Sophie's female lacrosse coach. Drew attacked the woman, and both kids were driven out of that school by the scandal."

Penny glanced at Moran. His jaw was clenched. He wouldn't meet her eye.

Penny whirled back to face Frank. "What difference does it make? Why are you digging into his personal life?"

"Don't you see? He had a motive to kill his wife. And he paid Tom Rayborn to pull the trigger. That's where Rayborn's money came from. He used the lottery ticket as a cover to explain his sudden wealth."

"You're the one who's talking crazy," Moran said. "My wife and I worked out our problems. I would never have hurt her. And

I don't even know this local man you're talking about."

Frank pulled Tom's cellphone from his pocket. "Then why does this number show up over and over in Tom Rayborn's recent calls? 908-555-3738—that's one digit off your personal cellphone number, isn't it? This is another one of your lines."

That brain--the brain that had blasted through MIT, the brain that had seen a problem and invented a product to solve it, the brain that had led a company and earned millions—that brain made the connection.

A second later, Frank's brain made it too: Drew's phone, Drew's plan.

A second too late. Moran lunged for Penny, catching her neck in the crook of his left arm. With his other hand, he snatched up the small knife lying on the cheese plate. He pressed it against the throbbing vein in Penny's slender neck.

Frank reached for his gun and Moran pressed the knife into Penny's skin. A tiny bright drop appeared at its tip.

Frank looked at what he was up against: a dull little paring knife. But the knife was ready and his gun would take precious seconds to draw. Plunged into a jugular, that knife could kill. An hour on snowy mountain roads to an ER—the risk was too great. His hand fell away from his gun.

Penny's eyes widened. She stopped struggling.

Frank had once talked a violent drunk into dropping the gun he was holding against his wife's temple. He hadn't thought it

S.W. Hubbard

required courage, just hyper-awareness. He tried now to summon the calm he'd used before. Not available.

He hadn't been in love with that other woman.

When he spoke his voice was sharp with fear. "You don't want to make this worse, Mike. You're a logical man. Let Penny go and we'll talk."

"I work with Wall Street traders, Bennett. I've learned one thing: you can't bargain from a position of weakness." He pulled Penny closer. "No one's going to ruin my son's future. Unbuckle your holster and put the whole thing up on that bookshelf."

Penny mewled like a kitten. Not enough air even to whimper.

Slowly, Frank did as he was told. Moran must not know how to use a gun, so he was taking it out of the equation. Very logical. He wasn't dealing with a mad man. The observation steadied him. His brain took a step back from his heart.

"Okay, Mike. You want to save your son. Any father would. Tell me what we need to do."

Frank saw the shock in Penny's eyes as she put together the pieces. She realized now that Drew had hired his mother's killer.

Moran nudged Penny. "Get my phone out of my shirt pocket and press the home button."

Penny got the phone and Moran gave a voice command, "Call Lance."

"Yo." The voice answered on the first ring.

"I need you to take me and the kids out tonight in the

chopper. Pick me up—Sophie can give you directions. Then line up Feinberg's plane."

"You got it."

Frank was impressed. That's what a billion dollar IPO bought—an assistant who didn't know the words "how" and "why". So Moran thought he could slip out of the country on a private jet. Let him try. Frank's anxiety wound down another notch. All he had to do was keep Moran calm until his assistant arrived. The state police and the FBI could easily track down a man on the lam with his kids. Frank's job was to keep Penny safe.

"Oh, Lance—tell the kids to pack light. There will actually be four of us flying."

The moments after Frank realized Moran planned to take Penny with him passed like the slow spiral of a car skidding into the path of a truck. Frank envisioned the plan: he would be incapacitated; Penny would be used to ensure the Morans' getaway. And then.... It was a crazy scheme, but Moran was an entrepreneur, a risk-taker. His success was built on ignoring people who told him his plans wouldn't work.

Right now, Moran held the high cards, but not yet the winning hand. He would never fold. Once Lance arrived, Frank's gun would come down from the shelf. No more cards would be dealt. Game over.

He had to act now.

Moran had grown weary of standing with his arm cocked at an awkward angle around Penny's neck. He lowered himself onto a straight-backed chair, forcing Penny to kneel in front of him. The knife never left her neck. Penny had stopped struggling. She watched Frank with the fixed attention of relay racer waiting for the baton.

Frank remained standing. He began to talk. "Kids are hard to predict, aren't they? You spend all your time watching for certain things—online predators, sketchy friends, booze—and then they come at you out of left field with something you never would have expected."

Moran stared past Frank, looking at the window where he expected to see Lance's headlights appearing in the driveway.

"Take my daughter." Frank edged toward the side table behind him. "Kid was a three-season athlete, healthy as a horse. Straight A student. Always had guys chasing her, so sex was what we worried about."

Moran didn't appear to be listening, but his breathing changed. Frank could hear every inhalation. He sized up his opponent. He and Moran were about the same size. Moran was a little younger, but he wasn't a brawler. Frank knew how to fight.

"One day the school called," Frank continued. "Teacher followed Caroline into the bathroom and caught her puking up her lunch. Bulimia." Frank shook his head. "Never saw that coming."

Moran allowed himself a quick glance in Frank's direction.

All Frank needed was a split second of distraction.

"She wouldn't go to a shrink, so the wife and I went. Turned out we were too controlling. We needed to give her more space. Seemed like crazy advice, but damned if it didn't work." Frank lowered his voice. "Did you realize how angry Drew was with his mother?"

"I...how could I—" Moran's left hand twitched in his lap, but the right hand still gripped the knife.

Frank needed a noise. Loud. Unfamiliar. He raised his hand as if to scratch his ear. An abstract metal sculpture on the table behind him clanged to the ground.

Penny flinched. Her captor started to stand.

Frank launched himself at Moran's shoulders. The delicate chair where he sat tipped over and all three of them tumbled to the ground, Penny sandwiched between the two men.

Frank struggled to pin Moran's knife-hand. The knife was no longer against Penny's neck, but Moran flailed wildly. Frank felt heat radiate from his jaw as the small blade caught him.

Penny screamed.

A plume of red stained her pale yellow sweater.

Fierce power propelled Frank. With his hip he pushed Penny out of the way and got his knees on Moran's chest. Even with both of his hands, he couldn't stop Moran's slashing. Hot blood ran into his eye. He didn't register pain.

He lunged again for Moran's right arm. The two men strained together, evenly matched, each fighting for what he loved.

Frank pried Moran's little finger away from the knife.

He twisted. They all heard the snap.

The knife fell to the floor.

The state police arrested Mike and Drew Moran; of course they lawyered up, so no information flowed there. Tom Rayborn, on the other hand, offered the state police's homicide investigators very little challenge. In the course of a few hours filled with threats, reassurances, and fried egg sandwiches, Tom moved from denial, to clumsy cover-up, to signed confession. Drew, Tom explained, had befriended Jeff and first pitched him with the idea of killing his mother in exchange for a sports car. Not knowing how to respond to his glamorous new friend, Jeff had come to his dad for advice. And Tom had accepted the job. With plenty of chemicals still coursing through his system, Tom was a little hazy on how Drew had worked the finances. All he knew was that Drew's father had taught him how to play the stock market starting in sixth grade, and by the time Drew turned eighteen, he controlled plenty of his own money.

Apart from a superficial scratch on her neck, Penny was uninjured. The blood on her sweater had come from Frank. Two EMTs had patched him up, warning that without stitches, the cut above his eye would leave a scar. He shrugged and kept working.

It took hours to process the crime scene at Penny's house. As state police officers and technicians combed through the living room, Penny holed up in her kitchen with a mug of tea and a Jane Austen novel whose pages she didn't turn.

"Let Earl take you over to the Iron Eagle," Frank begged for the third time.

Penny shook her head.

"I'll stop by later, when all this is finished."

"I'll just wait here until you're done."

"It could be hours. Please--Edwin will take care of you. Or I could call Pastor Bob."

Penny threw her book down. "Dammit, Frank! I don't want Edwin. I don't want Bob. I want you."

"Then why were you--" The words came out with a raw edge. Penny had already told him and the state police that Moran had come that night to get her advice on how to help Sophie. But that didn't fully explain the cozy scene he'd walked in on.

"What right do you have to be angry? You don't want me, but you don't want anyone else to want me either."

She was still wearing the stained sweater. Frank flashed on the rage he'd felt when he thought that blood had come from her heart. "Oh, Penny—can't you see how much I want you?" He put his hands on her shoulders, but kept her at arm's length. "I'm too old for you. You deserve the chance to have kids. I'm past that now."

She twisted out of his grasp. "I married Ned Stevenson to get what I thought he had: the perfect big happy family I'd always longed for. But you know what, Frank? There are no perfect families. We try to love the people we're supposed to love: mothers and fathers, sisters and brothers, daughters and sons. But stuff gets in the way. Disappointment. Greed. Jealousy. Desire. And the family that was supposed to always be there falls apart. There are no guarantees."

"That a pretty dark worldview."

"Not dark. Just realistic."

"Are you telling me you don't believe in the possibility of love? Of fidelity?"

Penny paced the kitchen, talking without making eye contact. "No, I believe people can love each other if they choose to, not if they're obliged to. But it seems like every link added to the family chain makes it weaker, not stronger. Parenthood is tremendously risky. Not everyone is cut out for it. Renee Moran shouldn't have been a mother. Tom Rayborn shouldn't have been a dad."

"Good lord, Penny—you're nothing like them! You're kind and generous and affectionate. You'd be a wonderful mother."

Penny shook her head. "Motherhood's not for me Frank. I'm not brave enough. I don't deal well with uncertainty. I just want to be Penny the loopy librarian. I want to introduce kids to the love of reading. I want to tell them stories and paint pictures with them. I want to show them how wide the world is. Then I want to send them back to their parents."

She came and stood before him. "And I want to lock the library door and go home. But I don't want to be alone."

Her voice dropped to a whisper. "I'm so alone."

Frank opened his arms.

They clung to each other. The only sound either one heard was the hard, steady beating of their hearts, not quite in sync.

If you enjoyed these Frank Bennett short stories, don't miss Frank's novel-length adventures: *The Lure, Blood Knot,* and *False Cast,* all available on amazon.com. Be sure to post a review!

ABOUT THE AUTHOR

S.W. Hubbard is the author of the Palmyrton Estate Sale Mystery Series, which takes place in a fictional town in New Jersey much like the one where she lives. She is also is the author of three mystery novels set in the Adirondack Mountains: *The Lure, Blood Knot,* and *False Cast.* Her short stories have appeared in *Alfred Hitchcock's Mystery Magazine* and the Mystery Writers of America anthologies *Crimes by Moonlight* and *The Mystery Box.* She lives in Morristown, NJ, where she teaches creative writing to enthusiastic teens and adults, and expository writing to reluctant college freshmen. Read the first chapters of all her books at http://www.swhubbard.net.

Made in the USA
Las Vegas, NV
05 April 2023

70199973R00069